INTERGALACTIC HEAT

BY

JESSICA E. SUBJECT

Featuring...

Beneath the Starry Sky
Celestial Seduction
Unknown Futures
Satin Sheets in Space
Sudden Breakaway

Decadent Publishing Company
www.decadentpublishing.com

This book is a work of fiction. Names, characters, places, and incidents are the products of the author's imagination or used fictitiously. Any resemblance to actual events, locales or persons, living or dead, is entirely coincidental.

Intergalactic Heat

ISBN: 978-1-61333-357-0
Cover design by Fantasia Frog and Cribley Designs

Published by Decadent Publishing Company
www.decadentpublishing.com

Printed in the United States of America

Beneath the Starry Sky

Chapter One

Tamara Johnson raced past the pretty, Latina concierge of the Castillo Hotel to the bathroom. The wig maker had assured her the suction wig would not come off in the wind and water, but she needed to check for herself. Driving with the window down hadn't been the brightest thing to do.

She brushed her hair back in place and found the wig had lived up to the claims. Well worth the price. Hopefully she could say the same thing tomorrow morning regarding the date she'd driven to the hotel for.

She hadn't planned to begin dating again, but her friend, Leah, managed to twist her arm. They'd met at a bakery the last time she'd come down to Vegas for work. "You're too fun to stay inside all the time," she had said. "Who cares if you don't have any hair? When you find the right guy it won't matter."

But it had mattered to her fiancé, Chad. Make that her *ex-fiancé*. He'd left her, claiming he couldn't marry a bald woman. His rejection had affected her so deeply that after steroid injections and several topical treatments proved unsuccessful, she'd looked to alternative medicine and paid a fortune for a radical new *natural* cream to treat her alopecia. That treatment turned her two small bald patches into a completely bald head.

With one last look at her wig, she took a deep breath and left the bathroom.

The concierge stood right outside the door, smirking, her eyebrows raised as if amused by her predicament. "Excuse me...."

If Leah hadn't taken Tamara to the hotel to meet her husband, Jackson, owner of the Castillo hotel chain—whom Leah had met during her own 1Night Stand—she wouldn't have even known where the restroom was. "I know I should have checked in first. I'm sorry. But I assure you I am a guest here."

"Yes, I was asked to personally escort you up to your guest room." The words rolled off her tongue in a lovely Spanish accent. "You're Miss Johnson, I presume?"

"You mean I don't need to check in?" How did this woman know who she was? She looked around for any sign of Leah, but she and Jackson had left the day before to look at a property in Ottawa, her hometown, for a new Castillo resort.

"That is correct, Miss Johnson. May I take your bag?"

So I don't back out.

She handed the overstuffed shoulder bag to the woman and followed her to the elevator. The silence chewed at her gut as they rode to the ninth floor. She had to say something before she lost the contents of her stomach. "My name is Tamara."

"Victoria." The woman reached out and shook her hand.

"So, how long have you worked here?"

Victoria's posture relaxed and she smiled. "Two years now."

"I'm sure you've seen a lot." She could only imagine the strange people who would come through the doors of any Vegas hotel. She'd seen a few on the city streets who'd made her look twice.

"Yes, I have." Victoria laughed. "It makes the job interesting."

Arriving at her room, Tamara took her bag back and tipped the woman well. "Thank you and have a good night."

"And you as well, Miss Johnson."

Entering the large suite, she searched for any sign of her date. Madame Evangeline hadn't given her any details, only that she would meet him at the hotel. Her stomach had been twisted in knots all day thinking of the possibilities. She found no one else in the room, but a welcome card sat on the king-size bed beside a box of chocolates.

Dear Tamara,

Your date for the evening will arrive soon. Please make yourself comfortable while you wait. A word of advice; don't be afraid to show him the real you.

Enjoy your evening,
Madame Evangeline

She threw the note back on the bed. *The real me?* She didn't even know who that was anymore.

Didn't matter. The date would only last one night. Sure, Leah had found Jackson, but Tamara hadn't come on the date looking for love. She only wanted a night of passion, a night to prove she could date again, even hidden under her wig. Love meant taking the wig off and she would never expose her bald head to a man again. If that meant a life of one-night stands, so be it.

She reached into her shoulder bag and pulled out the red lace teddy she'd bought the day before. *If there's one way to get a man to fuck me, it's with sexy lingerie.*

After changing into the form-fitting outfit, she waited on the bed, trying to figure out the sexiest pose to be in when her date arrived. *What says 'take me now?'*

Josh Summers rushed through the doors of the Castillo Hotel. He'd come to Vegas to finally escape the big city and bright lights, at least the one where crazed fans and paparazzi followed him everywhere. Unfortunately they followed him to Vegas. Thankfully, Castillo hotels and resorts had a reputation for keeping out those he constantly tried to avoid. But it also meant he had to miss the meteor shower that night. The stars of Hollywood could never compare to the celestial wonders in the sky. It had taken him years to notice there was more to life than bright lights, dollar signs, and hot women. He'd had plenty of them all, until his accident. That moment and the following months had opened his eyes to the reality of the world he'd been living in. Friends were only friends as long as he kept making money. And the women he'd trusted after the event that left him scarred had only wanted him until they saw his now imperfect body up close. Many in a similar position would have turned to drugs, but he'd escaped to the outdoors, finding peace and acceptance in the solitude. Sure, he'd kept the accident a secret from the tabloids, consenting to an out of court settlement and paying a ludicrous price for hair transplant surgery, but refusing to take his shirt off reduced the number of acting contracts he was offered. And with his current contract now expired, he'd failed to sign a new one.

His fans though, did not know about the accident that left his body damaged. He'd let them keep their fantasies instead of being featured in their nightmares. Yet, on days like this one, when he'd been sideswiped by flashing cameras in between leaving his car with the valet and stepping into the hotel, he considered showing them the monster he'd become. No, as long as he stayed inside, he would be safe for the next ten days while contractors finished the renovations to his new home and Kevin Keinelburt decided whether he wanted to invest in his new production company. The business proposition would take him out of the spotlight to behind-the-scenes. And out of the tabloids. He checked in then grabbed a protein bar from his bag to eat while riding in the elevator.

He wanted to relax. Even though the network hadn't renewed his contract and ended his television series after two seasons, he still had months of promo after the last episode aired. They had to thank the fans. Unfortunately for the entire cast, some people didn't know the difference between being a fan and a stalker. But Josh noticed it the most. His stalkers, claiming to be fans, attempted to rip off chunks of his clothing and chipped paint off of his car. Paparazzi weren't afraid to get *in* his car.

Ten days locked in a hotel will be the best holiday ever. I won't have to keep myself covered. I'm free to walk around naked if I want.

He set his bag down to slide the key card in the lock. Pushing the door open, he entered his room. Ready to crash on the bed, he tossed his keys, phone and wallet on the counter in the kitchenette then he slipped off his shoes and socks.

He reached for the light switch on the bedroom wall and heard the bed shift. *Fuck!* Who was in his room?

Light flooded the room and he jumped back, seeing a woman on his bed. A very sexy, scantily-clad woman lying across the sheets in a provocative position. But that woman wasn't supposed to be in his room.

Maybe the attendant at the front desk had incorrectly programmed his key card. "I'm sorry, ma'am. I didn't mean to walk in on you. There must have been some mistake." Thinking she was a stalker would only ruin his stay at the hotel.

"Um, aren't you...?"

"Josh Summers? Yes, sorry, I'll go back down and get this figured out."

When she sat up, her smile dropped in disappointment. "Who? No, I thought you were my date."

He backed out of the room. "I'm sorry, but I'm not him. He sure is one lucky guy though. Have a good evening."

Rounding up all of his belongings, he couldn't get out of the suite fast enough. Sure, the woman was gorgeous with her long, honey-colored hair, perfectly-rounded curves, kissable red-painted lips.... But she looked like every other girl he'd previously dated, with her flawless hair and makeup—high-maintenance. And sure to make a quick exit at the sight of his back.

His new spur of the moment nature didn't mesh well with those women who spent hours in front of the mirror to go for a walk. Someone would get lucky tonight, but not him. He wanted to be alone.

Walking toward the elevator, his cell phone chimed with a text message.

Good evening, Joshua. I trust you've made it to the Castillo without losing a limb?

Only one person called him Joshua, and it wasn't his mother. But the phone number attached to the text did not belong to his older brother either. *Madame Evangeline.* Yet another unwelcome surprise.

To what do I owe the pleasure?

Why, we have unfinished business.

I thought you had a no refund policy. The money he'd spent for Madame Evangeline's 1Night Stand dating service had gone to waste. If only he'd known his brother was gay before he contacted her.

Yes, if only you'd known your brother was already engaged to Kyle before you set him up?

How did you...?

Another message came in before he'd hit send. *The policy remains, but that does not mean the payment cannot be transferred to someone else.*

No, no, no!

Your brother contacted me the other day. He seemed concerned about you.

He slammed his fist against the wall before sending a message back. *What are you telling me?*

The beautiful woman in your suite is waiting to spend the evening in your company.

He groaned, fighting the urge to throw his phone on the ground and stomp on it. Yes, he'd tried to set his brother up on a date, but he would never consider that kind of service for himself. And this was supposed to be his time to himself. Alone. *No, I never applied to your dating service. I'm not even looking for a relationship right now.*

If only you believed your own words. She is exactly what you are looking for.

Most of the women he encountered, including the mob outside, believed they were exactly what he was looking for because they'd followed the tabloids from his early career or read his profile on the *Searching For Earth* fan site. But that profile matched his character, not him anymore. If the woman in his room had been on SFE, his character would definitely spend the night with her. But *he* needed a different type of woman.

I believe your brother knows you better than those fan sites. Come now. It's only one night.

How did she get into his head? *I know how you work. You don't set just anyone up. That's why I chose you to set up Trevor.*

Then you know I didn't take the task of finding your date lightly. Now, are you up for an evening of fun, or shall I inform the lovely woman you're not interested?

If only he was more like his character, like his former self. *I'll return to my room, but I think you've made a mistake.*

I never make mistakes. Have a wonderful evening.

Wait, what's her name? But his text went unanswered.

Trevor was going to pay the next time he saw him.

Tamara slid off the red lace and tossed it back in the bag. Why did she think she could hide under the wig? Even the guy who'd mistakenly entered her suite hadn't shown her any sign she was desirable. He'd seen through her disguise and couldn't get out of the room fast enough.

He'd been drop-dead gorgeous, too. With tanned, perfect skin, and a gym-toned body, he could be a part of her fantasies any day. But he hadn't wanted her. No man would, ever again. They saw her as nothing but a freak.

Her date wasn't coming; she'd waited over an hour already. He'd probably looked her up on Facebook and seen a picture of her with her bald head, then changed his mind.

Slipping her fingers underneath the edge of her wig, she broke the seal and tossed the display of hair across the room. Her enraged scream echoed off the walls. Tears fell. She'd be alone forever because of the incurable autoimmune disease invading her body.

Flopping onto the bed, she curled up into a ball, unable to face going home. But she couldn't stay there by herself either.

"Hello?"

She sat up, her heart pounding. *Shit!* Someone else had come into the suite and there she sat, naked. No hair, no clothes, nothing.

Footsteps padded toward the room. She had to get dressed. Her clothes sat on the floor by the bed, but she had no idea where her wig had landed. The footsteps grew closer. She dove over the bed, hoping to find the wig on the other side, taking her little black dress with her. *Shit! Where's my hair? Why can't I just be normal?*

"Hello, is anyone here?"

She had enough time to throw on the dress *sans* bra and thong before he was in the room with her.

The same man from before stared at her from the doorway. What was his name? Josh?

And she stood there, exposed. With a bald head, and makeup surely running down her face from all the crying.

With his mouth hanging open, his eyes grew wide, the collection of multi-colored roses held in his hand taking a nosedive for the floor.

Oh, God! She'd held onto so much hope for this date, and nothing had gone right. She still didn't know who this guy was. Yet, he'd already rejected her with his expression. *This is the last date I'm going on, unless I'm lucky enough for my hair to grow back.*

His gaze never left her, making her even more humiliated. "You're...."

"What? Ugly? Bald?"

He shook his head. "No, I was going to say my date. I've been so busy lately and Madame Evangeline had to send me a reminder."

She paused at the Frenchwoman's name. Could this hunk of a man really be her date? Didn't matter. He wouldn't want her now. "Well, surprise! I'm damaged goods, so you might as well leave and ask her for a refund."

As she slumped to the floor, more tears streamed down her face. *Why is life so unfair?* She'd worked hard all of her life, never taking shortcuts or the easy way out. Not an outcast or popular, she'd been friends with everyone in school and college. And healthy. She'd taken extra care to eat properly in order to avoid being diagnosed with diabetes, like her parents.

Since that fateful day when she'd discovered her two, oval-shaped bald patches, she'd been dumped by her fiancé and lost all of her hair, along with any chance to find love and have a family vanishing. Kids were out of the question. Sure, their chances of inheriting alopecia were unlikely, but on the chance they did, they'd hate her for passing her faulty genetics on to them. She couldn't live with that. She'd be alone. Forever.

He loomed over her.

"What do you want?" She couldn't look at him, couldn't stand to see the disgust he surely felt from being set up with her.

"I found your wig." He sat beside her on the floor, placing the tangle of hair on her lap.

"Thanks. You can leave. I just want to be alone." She might as well get started now.

"I thought we had a date."

She heard no revulsion in his voice and glanced over at him. "You still want to have a one-night stand with me after seeing me like this?" *Is this guy blind?*

"Sure. It's not very often I find someone who I can relate to. What's your name? Madame Eve never told me."

She tensed. "Tamara. But you know nothing about me or what I'm going through." She stood up. If he wasn't going to leave, she would.

As she walked past, he grabbed her arm. "I *can* relate, and I'll show you if you just give me a chance."

Too weak to fight from all of her crying, she didn't resist. "Fine, show me."

He released her then unbuttoned his shirt and took it off. Turning around, he said, "Look at my back. See all of the scarring there? Well, it extends up past my hairline. I went with hair restoration surgery instead of a wig, but I still know what the sting of rejection feels like."

Her eyes widened. *Insert foot in mouth.* "I'm sorry." She'd acted like a bitch, and the last thing he needed was more rejection, more people feeling sorry for him. If anything, they both needed someone who could simply understand. "It's just that so many people sympathize with how I feel, but they truly have no idea what it's like to have alopecia, to have hair one day and none the next."

He drew in a deep breath. "I know."

Trailing a finger over the ridges and valleys of his scarred skin, she let go of all of the animosity she'd built up. "I guess you would. How did it happen?"

"It was a pyrotechnics accident." He sat on the bed and patted the sheets.

She joined him, curious to know more about her mysterious date.

"I used to be a model before I was an actor. During a private shoot, a flare ignited prematurely. It came at me from the side and burnt my back." He cringed as if he could still feel the pain of the experience. "I settled out of court to keep it from the media, but I had to give up modeling. With the settlement, I went for the hair transplant then went into acting instead."

"You're an actor?" That would explain his good looks, his chiseled body. How had she landed a date with a man like him? Sure, he had scars, but still....

"Yes, but let's not talk about that. Why don't you go to the bathroom and wash up so we can begin our date?"

Wiping her eyes, she noticed streaks of mascara on her hands. "I must look pretty awful."

He brushed his hand across her arm. "No, you look beautiful, but you're hiding your beauty under all of that makeup." He wrapped his arm around her back, drawing her into him. The captivating scent of sandalwood and pure masculinity filled her. "Tamara, I'm sorry for being late tonight. Will you accept my apology?"

She gazed into his brown eyes, ready to melt. "Yes."

He kissed her forehead before letting her go, making her

knees quiver. "Perfect. Now, get going so we can get to know each other better."

She rushed to the washroom, using the opportunity to figure out the situation. Had they been set up together because they were both damaged? Yes, he had scars, but would he really want to spend the night with a bald woman? He could still get any girl he wanted.

She cringed as she took in her reflection in the mirror. *Beautiful? Yeah, right!* Mascara lines decorated her face from her red-rimmed eyes, down to her chin. Snot pooled underneath her nose. *What is this guy playing at?* He probably sent her to the bathroom as a chance to escape.

Splashing water on her face, she then used a cloth to wipe off her make-up artist's tear-ruined masterpiece. She dried off her face then secured her wig. There was no way she would face him again, bald. She couldn't stand to see the little exclamation point hairs which sprouted here and there. Why would he find that attractive? Yet when she left the bathroom, she couldn't help but expect to find the suite empty.

Josh watched the firm ass of his date as she walked toward the bathroom. She definitely held his eye, bald head and all, but would she keep his attention? Would she keep up with him?

God, he hoped so. With only one way to find out—a field trip—he picked up the phone.

Shit! The Planetarium at the College of Southern Nevada had already closed. What kind of star-gazing facility closed early on the night of a big meteor shower? Carson City was too far away. The only other option meant sacrificing his privacy, something he valued over everything.

Had Madame Evangeline really found his ideal date? For some crazy reason, even though she'd ruined his night, he resolved to trust the mysterious woman. Changing into sweatpants and a T-shirt, he threw on some socks, found his running shoes, then waited for Tamara to come out. *Maybe this date won't be so bad.* She hadn't run away when she'd seen his scars—instead she'd touched them.

When the door opened, he took pleasure in her nervous apprehension.

"Hi," she squeaked, like a teenage girl on her first date.

He approached her, holding out his hand. "Let's do this properly. I'm Josh Summers, your date for this evening."

She reached for his hand. Instead of shaking hers, he brought it to his lips for a kiss.

She blushed, making her even more appealing. "I'm, ah...Tamara, Tamara Johnson."

"Well, Miss Johnson, if it is okay with you, I'd like to take you out of the hotel to one of my favorite places to visit."

He still held onto her hand and she made no motion to pull away. "Um, I don't think I can, not without...."

Interrupting her next words, he leaned in and kissed her lips then quickly pulled away. "Without what? You already have your wig on, which was unnecessary, but you will need more comfortable clothing." He led her over to the side of the bed where her bag sat. "What do you have?"

She chewed on her bottom lip, and he wanted to taste those sweet lips again.

"Only what I'm wearing and what you saw me in earlier."

"We'll have to take care of that then. Let's go down to the gym and see what they have." He hooked his arm around hers but she resisted, not moving.

"I ah, need to put something else on before we go."

"What else could you need? Don't tell me you're one of those women who can't leave the house without makeup." He turned toward her, placing his hands on her arms. "Tamara, you're beautiful without it."

Her cheeks reddened once more.

"No, I need to put these on." She reached into her bag and pulled out her matching red lace bra and panties.

Thoughts of her wearing nothing under her short, black dress made him instantly hard. If she bent over, he'd have full view of her sweet spot.

He had to leave the room before he took her right there on the bed. The date mattered too much to ruin it with instant sex. There'd be time enough for that later, after he showed her another part of himself only a select few ever saw. "I'll let you put those back on. Meet me at the front door when you're ready."

Chapter Two

He walked away, leaving her confused. One minute Josh had his hands on her, sending desire coursing through her body, then the next he left for the other room. He'd flushed though, when she'd told him she wasn't wearing any underwear. Why hadn't he done anything about it?

But he'd told her she was beautiful. He'd looked directly into her eyes when he'd said the word. And she began to believe him. But had he meant it when she hadn't been wearing her wig?

She slipped her thong back on. Should she trust the gorgeous hunk she'd been set up with? Spending time with a man who made her feel more confident would do her some good. She couldn't feel any worse. But would he change his mind? Her stomach sank, remembering how her fiancé had once supported her too, until he changed *his* mind.

She had to get moving before she lost her confidence. Grabbing her bag, she walked out of the room to meet her one-night stand. He grinned at her, the way she'd imagined her fiancé would on the day they married. What could this guy possibly see in her? "I'm ready to go."

He placed his arm around her back, his hand resting on her side, and guided her out of the suite. "Great. Let's get you some more appropriate clothes for our date."

She laughed, the first time she'd laughed around any man in

months. How were the sweats he wore appropriate for a date? "Where exactly are we going?"

He turned toward her as they waited for the elevator. His hands held hers. "I want it to be a surprise. It's a place really special to me."

His soft, soothing voice made her melt. Why would he take her to his special place when they were still strangers? Did he expect more than a one-night stand or was he some crazed killer claiming to be an actor, and wanting to take her away from the hotel to dispose of her soon-to-be lifeless body? Surely Madame Evangeline screened everyone before setting them up, but the doubt had already implanted in her mind. She slipped away from him as the elevator door opened.

He stepped inside, but her apprehension kept her feet planted firmly in the hall.

He reached out toward her. "Are you coming?"

"I...I've changed my mind. I don't want to leave the hotel room." She only wanted to have sex, not go on some grand adventure with some guy she didn't know. But yet she was willing to have sex with this stranger? *God, what is wrong with me?*

Leaving the elevator, he wrapped his arms around her, capturing her mouth with hungry urgency. She responded without conscious thought. Her mind numbed, only filled with her date as his lips and tongue set on a quest to weaken her. She floated into the elevator, felt the car descending, but could do nothing to stop their travels. She didn't want to. If being in his arms, having him kiss her, always made her forget her problems and the rest of the world, she'd stay there forever.

He pulled away, leaving her gasping for air.

"Are we...leaving the hotel?"

His lips curved into the sexiest damn smile she'd ever seen. "Don't you trust me?"

She hesitated. She had to trust him in some ways, but.... "I don't even know you."

Brushing his fingers across her cheek, he kept her weak. "You really have never heard of me before?"

What was that supposed to mean? "No, should I have?"

He laughed. "No, I like it better this way. But you can trust me. I'm trusting you're telling me the truth and aren't some crazed fan."

Crazed fan? "Okay, now you have to tell me."

The elevator doors opened and he took her hand, guiding her across the hall to the gym's boutique. "What are your measurements?"

She still waited for an answer to her last question. "Pardon?"

"Your size. You need shoes and clothes."

Self-conscious of the other patrons knowing those personal details, she leaned in and whispered them to him. He dropped her hand and made his way around the boutique, throwing clothes over his arm. He returned to her and placed the clothing and a box in her arms. "Go try these on."

The clothes fit like a second skin, literally, but not to the point she couldn't breathe. She grabbed the door handle of the dressing room, needing to look at herself in the mirror. Why couldn't mirrors be *in* dressing rooms anymore?

As soon as she opened the door, he spun her into his arms. Instead of another kiss, he ripped the tags off the clothes and set them on the counter. "Charge them to my room." He grabbed her hand and yanked her out of the boutique.

If she hadn't seen the fear in his eyes, she would have been pissed that he pulled her with so much force. "What's going on? My other clothes are still in the other room."

He slowed his pace, but didn't stop. "I'm sorry, Tamara, but we've got to leave, now."

The pretty concierge appeared before them. "Mr. Summers, can I have someone get your car for you?"

"Thank you, Victoria, but I'll get it myself from the garage. Could you possibly retrieve Tamara's clothes from the dressing room of the boutique and take them back to my room?"

"Sure thing." Victoria handed him his keys. They continued through the hall then down the stairs, her new shoes barely touching the ground.

Who the hell is this guy and what are we running from?

Shit! I can't go anywhere without someone getting out their camera. He raced with Tamara in tow, trying to keep her from the intrusive life he lived. He wasn't ready to bring anyone into the spotlight with him yet.

But he had to get out of the hotel first. He unlocked his car and held the door open for her. Even when trying to beat the paparazzi, he still believed in chivalry. After shoving her inside a bit too roughly, he muttered an apology, closed her door then rushed around to the driver's side. Throwing the car in reverse, he squealed the tires in a rush to get out of the parking garage. How much time did he have? He didn't know, but if the paparazzi followed him, he'd have to pull some fancy maneuvers to lose them before driving to his destination.

They made it to the street before he was temporarily blinded by the first flashes. Tamara shrieked when someone knocked on her window, right before another flash of light.

Fuck! I have to get away from this, get her away from this.

Pulling onto the Strip, he expected them to stop, leave him alone. But another photographer jumped onto the hood. Josh closed his eyes so the upcoming flash wouldn't leave him sightless and slammed on the brakes. The man flew off. He made sure the crazy paparazzo was out of the way before taking off. The last thing he needed was to be sued by some maniac with a camera.

When he'd finally made it off the Strip and onto darker streets, he released the breath he'd held.

"Who the hell are you?"

Her words were mixed with fear and anger. With a glassy stare, she waited for his answer. Would the truth ruin what could have been? If he didn't tell her, she could Google his name anyway.

"I told you I'm an actor, or at least I was, and a former model. The show I'd been on for two years was recently canceled."

Her eyes softened. "But why are people following you? Are you really that famous?"

He laughed. "Obviously not if you've never heard of me. But when you're an underwear model, you get obsessive fans, and then I was on *Searching For Earth* on the sci-fi channel. Don't you follow the tabloids?"

"No, I have better things to do, but I may have to start watching the sci-fi channel if all the actors are as hot as you."

All tension from the encounter with the paparazzi diminished when he saw her smile. He reached over and squeezed her thigh. "Maybe you shouldn't. They're all known to be players."

She placed her hand on his, making him want to touch even more of her. "Yourself included?"

He heard the playful tone of her voice, but he wouldn't make her think he had a big ego. "Maybe at one time, but things changed after the accident. I'm sure you understand."

She nodded. "So now that your show's done, what are you doing next?"

He told her about his plans to become a film producer. She told him about the pharmaceutical company she worked for, and all of the places she traveled on business. They spent the entire hour talking, with no awkward silences. By the time he pulled into the driveway of his future house, thoughts of her naked body pressed against his had taken over his mind. It had been so long since he'd been with anyone, let alone a down-to-earth woman who he could relate to and vice versa. Not only could he see himself driving his already hard shaft into her, but also walking alongside her, holding hands and talking. Conversation had not been a forte of many of his previous dates. *Maybe Madame Evangeline does know what she's doing.* But they hadn't yet reached their destination. He had time to figure out whether she wanted him as much as he wanted her.

Staring at the wide expanse of a house in front of her, Tamara's jaw hung open. *Shut your mouth before you start drooling. It's just a house.*

But the building was more than that—it was the home of her dreams. The Mediterranean-style exterior stood out amongst the ponderosa pines and white fir trees standing tall behind the house. She couldn't imagine living in a house so secluded from the civilization, yet close enough that a jaunt into the city wouldn't be a day trip. How could anyone afford such a masterpiece? Her condo already cost a fortune. "Whose house is this?"

Josh's hand remained on her thigh. She didn't want him to stop touching her, but the console prevented her from getting any closer.

"It's my house. I'll be moving in once the renovations are complete."

"It's gorgeous, but do you think it's big enough?" She watched the smile spread all the way up to his eyes. She'd seen it more often, replacing his scowl, as they'd driven closer to his house and she learned more about him. What did her superstar have in store for her?

"I hope to one day have more people to share it with, but until then...." Without finishing his thought, he released her leg and got out of the car to rush over and open the door for her. She appreciated a man with old-school values. Her parents would call him a *keeper*. But Chad had once been that way, too.

She shook her head. *No more thoughts about him. It's time to move on.* As soon as he had her out of the car, Josh walked around to the trunk and pulled out a backpack fitted with a foam mat and sleeping bag underneath. He set it onto his shoulders and buckled the snaps at the front.

"I take it you don't have any furniture inside?" She gestured toward the house. Sure, she wanted to see the interior of his house, but sleeping on the floor held no appeal, foam mat or not.

"No, I don't." He turned toward her and took her hand before leading her past the house. "But that's not our destination."

They were going into the forest? She hadn't been hiking for years. Not that she didn't enjoy nature, but between wedding plans then immersing herself in her work after the break-up, she hadn't found the time. Josh reminded her of everything she used to be, before she lost her hair. And there she was with an extremely sexy guy who seemed happy to be in her company. But only for one night. Then they would part ways and she'd be left alone. And still bald.

Tripping over a rock on the path, she fell forward, the ground rushing toward her. She put her hands out to stop her fall, but Josh pulled her back up and against his body before she hit dirt.

He brushed her hair out of her mouth. "Careful. Don't let that rock push you around."

She punched his arm playfully, but his finger became tangled in her wig. As he tugged, her wig lost suction and fell to the ground.

They both jumped back and she gasped.

"Why do you hide under that thing?" He tilted her head up, but she couldn't look into his eyes. Not when she was so exposed.

"Because I'm a freak."

Shaking his head, he brushed his fingers across her cheek. "No, you're beautiful. Even more so now that I can see the real you again."

"How can I be beautiful when I have no hair, only bristly points which are likely to fall out?"

He pulled her back into his arms. "When you look at me, do you see a freak, a monster?"

"No." How could he even think that about himself? He was the most gorgeous man she had ever seen. For the next month, hopefully longer, he'd be the star of her fantasies.

"Well, I feel the same about you. It doesn't matter to me that you're bald. I can see past that. Maybe others feel differently, but it's only the two of us out here." He brushed his lips across her neck. "In fact, I'd like to see the rest of you just as bare."

A chill ran down her spine. She looked up at him, every part of her hoping she'd heard him correctly. *Can this really be happening? Does he really not care that I'm bald?*

"Now, you fell because you were lost in your thoughts. Did they have anything to do with me?" He wiggled his eyebrows, bringing a smile to her face. She hadn't smiled without her wig on, ever.

"Maybe...." The situation was all too much to take. Nothing

had gone as she'd expected. She needed to think. Turning out of his arms, she walked further up the path.

"Hey," he called after her. "Get back here. I'm not done rescuing you yet."

But she only wanted to run. "I guess you'll have to catch me then." She took off, this time watching where she placed her feet. The air blew past her cheeks, over her bald head, and she rediscovered her long lost freedom. Even as he chased her, she could not deny the exhilaration of finding herself again. Of being accepted. She didn't dare look back to see where he was, but she heard the pounding of his feet not far behind her. "So much for my hero."

The pine and fir trees thinned out, giving way to more rock. A wall of limestone ran along one side of the path, the occasional bristle cones on the other, beauty she'd lost in the depths of the cities she'd spent her days in.

A hand grabbed her arm. "Your mind started to wander again. You slowed down." He backed her against the side of the mountain, his hands on either side of her head. "Now it's time to finish rescuing you."

He snapped open the backpack buckles and let it fall to the ground, before his lips were on hers. He kept his kisses light, but she wanted more. She pulled him closer, her body pressed between a wall of rock and one of muscle and masculinity. His kisses deepened and his tongue probed for an opening. She granted him access, her own tongue plunging for a deeper connection.

She moaned into his mouth as his hands travelled up her shirt, cupping each breast, her bra still on the dressing room floor. Never before had she had sex outside, but now was as good a time as any. His hard member pressed against her stomach, but she didn't want the clothing between them any longer. Slipping her hands under his shirt, she lifted it off. He had hers off in one swift motion.

"Tamara," he whispered, his broad, firm chest pressed against her bare breasts. "I want you. We're not there yet, but I want you now."

Chapter Three

He'd tried to resist her, but her sweet vulnerability made him crazy. He ached for her, had to feel her sweet juices around his hard cock. Adrenaline pumped through his body from chasing after her, and it would continue with every deep thrust inside of her. He yanked her pants down and tore off the thin scrap of material she used as underwear, now damp from her arousal.

"Oh, Josh." She shuddered.

Could he get any harder? She'd stepped out of her pants already and he rushed to get out of his.

Her hand cupped his balls, squeezing, caressing until he was ready to come in her hand. *God no, it's way too soon.*

He removed her hand and joined it with the other to hold them above her head. With his free hand, he slid a finger inside her wet pussy. Then two fingers.

Her moans encouraged him to plunge deeper, harder, until the need to have his aching shaft inside of her overcame him. He removed his fingers and sucked off her juices. "You taste so good. I'm going to fuck you now."

He wanted to take his time with her, seduce her, and savor her, but not this time. Not when the need to feel her pulsing core around him was the only thing on his mind.

"Do you have a condom?" Her words came out as a seductive

whisper, as if she'd asked him to fuck her.

Shit! He hadn't thought that far ahead. *The backpack. There might be some in there.* But then he'd have to let her go. He didn't want to break contact, but he needed his cock buried deep inside of her.

Releasing her arms, he became aware of the cooler air in the higher elevation. He'd have to hurry before he lost his erection. He fished into the bag, sure he'd packed some in there for a date months earlier, one that had ended with rejection before it even began. *Don't think of that right now.* He frantically pawed through the contents. *Please, please!* His fingers wrapped around a familiar package, he yanked out the foil wrapper, and tore the edge open with shaky hands. *Thank God.*

"Do you always carry condoms?" He wasn't sure if she meant to be playful, though he sensed a hint of insecurity in her question.

"When in the woods, one must always be prepared."

Taking the condom from him, she smiled. "Well, I'm glad you paid attention in Boy Scouts." After sheathing him, she bent down. Her mouth encircled his shaft.

When she took him all the way in and swallowed, his knees nearly buckled. He pulled her back up. "Tamara, as much as I love your mouth around my cock, I have to stop you. I need to be inside of you."

She pressed her body against him, her sweet lips reaching up to his. He could lose his mind in her passionate, desperate kisses. He reached down to play with her wet core before lifting her legs around his waist. The tip of his cock met her slippery softness.

"Fuck me, Josh. I want you now." She'd lost the sweet, seductive tone. Her words held a demand.

He speared her, her wet warmth tightening all around him. Her head fell back, but he couldn't have that. He wanted to watch her as he sank deep, stroke after stroke. Stepping closer to the wall of rock, he pressed her against it, forcing her head back up.

"Look at me. I want to watch you as I fuck you."

Her eyes widened with each stroke. Her muscles pulsed, gripping him harder each time, bringing him closer to his own release. But he would never be selfish with her. The date was for her.

"Josh?"

He slowed his pace. "Hmm?"

"I want your eyes open, too."

He hadn't realized he'd closed them. She smiled at him right before she came. Her muscles clenched around his cock, her fingers dug into his arms and he continued to pump into her.

So close. She still had a firm hold on him, her muscles refusing to relax.

"Are you ready for another?" he asked with a hard thrust.

She moaned in response, her release taking him over. Her pussy milked him as he leaned against her, both of them using the rock for support.

When he caught his breath, he licked her sweet, yet salty neck. Gone was the flowery scent from their first meeting, replaced by the smell of sex. He still wanted to taste every part of her, but not there.

They only had a few minutes of daylight left. He had to get her to the cave before they lost all light; a flashlight could only do so much.

The cave.... He'd always imagined making love to a woman there, of taking her to watch a meteor shower before creating stars of their own as he worshiped every inch of her body. And now he would.

Stepping back, he lowered her to the ground, and made sure she stood steady on her feet before letting her go. "Tamara, you are amazing. I want to do that again, but we've only got a short period of time to get to our destination."

She tilted her head to the side. "Where are we going? What else do you have planned?"

"It's a surprise." And he couldn't wait to show her.

Her back ached where the rock had dug in, but Tamara couldn't have cared less as they dressed. Outdoor sex, against a wall, with a guy who satisfied her in every way? And he hadn't even cared that she had no hair. Nothing could be more perfect. She couldn't wait to find out what else he had in store for her.

He strapped on the backpack and took her hand. "Let's go. It's only a twenty minute hike from here." Then he smiled, his eyes revealing a secret within. If only she could figure it out. "No running this time. There are too many loose rocks. I have plans for you and they don't involve taking you to the hospital."

A chill of excitement rushed through her, making her want to run again. He must have sensed her anticipation as he squeezed her hand. "Good things come to those who are patient."

Her life had been full of waiting; waiting for a diagnosis, waiting for her hair to grow back, waiting for Chad to change his mind, waiting to find her *true* love.... The date would only last one night. She wanted to get as much fun in as she could without having to wait.

She pulled him along the trail, expecting him to stop her if she went the wrong way. Every time she'd look back at him, hoping to encourage him to move faster, he'd give her a devious grin.

She tried to speed up, but when he stopped cold, she almost fell over again. Staring at him, she rested her hands on her hips. "I thought we had to hurry and get to this destination of yours."

"We do, but I'd like you to save some of this energy for later on. I want to be the one to take your breath away." He flashed another grin before lifting her up and over his shoulder.

Afraid they would both fall over if she squirmed, she could only laugh. "Really? Can you carry all this extra weight?" She wasn't big, but she wasn't tiny either. He may want to take her breath away, but he couldn't do so if he wrenched his back.

"Well, the backpack's a little heavy, but you're light as a feather." He tapped her ass, making her squeal.

The morning would be difficult. The date was proving more fun than she'd expected. She'd smiled so much her cheeks ached, had hot sex against a wall of rock and waited anxiously atop his shoulder to find out what else he had planned.

But how would she say goodbye in the morning?

They stopped and he set her back down on the ground. She

gasped, taking in the scenery visible in the twilight. Water seeped down the cliff face on her right. To the left, she saw the last of the sun's rays shining overtop the array of pines down the mountainside. "It's beautiful."

"Just like you." He took her hand in his. "I thought you would enjoy it here, but this is only the beginning."

"What do you mean?" What other surprises did he have in store?

He pulled the flashlight out from his backpack and shone it upon rock, to the side of the trickling waterfall. "Do you see the cave up there?"

She nodded, spotting the black hole twenty feet above the ground.

"That's where we're going to spend the rest of the night. I'll show you the surprise from up there."

With the sun now set, a cool breeze swept across the mountainside, making her shiver. She didn't even have her wig to keep her warm. Josh had stuffed it in the backpack and refused to give it back. From behind, he wrapped his arms around her. "Trust me; you won't be cold for long."

Her breath hitched as his lips trailed kisses up her neck. When he found the spot right below her ear, her knees buckled, but he held onto her.

How am I going to say goodbye to him in the morning when he makes me feel so damn good?

He spun her around to face him. "Are you ready to climb up there?"

With his hands firmly on her ass, he helped Tamara climb up to the cave. "You're almost there. Just a couple more feet."

When she reached the top, she left him empty-handed. Even though she stood a few feet above him, he longed to touch her again, to run his hands over her soft curves. He sure as hell didn't believe in love at first sight, but the woman had captivated him in only a few hours. With the morning though, would come uncertainty. Until then, he would savor every second in her presence.

Hoisting the backpack up to her, he caught a glimpse of her ample cleavage. His cock stiffened immediately. He wanted to taste her glistening breasts, taste all of her.

By the time he reached the top, she had already taken his backpack to the rear of the cave. The mat lay on the ground, and she unrolled his sleeping bag across it.

He could have stood there and watched her forever, but his hands, mouth and cock wanted to experience her again. "Tamara, as much as I enjoy watching you bent over, I'm going to have to bring that over here. We need to be closer to the edge."

"The edge?" A look of terror flashed across her face. "What if we fall off?"

He laughed then helped her up, into his arms. "I don't plan on letting you fall over. Besides, the show is going to start soon."

Her wide eyes stared up at him. "What show?"

"Let's move and find out." He pulled the foam mat and sleeping bag to the entrance of the cave. Sitting down on the bag, he settled her between his legs. He flicked the flashlight off and stared up at the sky.

The first flash of light shot across the indigo background. She gasped. "That was a shooting star."

He held her tighter. "That's only the beginning. There'll be plenty of wishes made tonight and I hope I can grant some of them for you." Kissing the back of her bare head, he smiled when she gave in, relaxed against him.

The stars could wait....

Tamara could not have asked for a better night. She'd been nervous about leaving the hotel, but the evening had been well worth the anxiety of him catching her bald and their escape from the paparazzi. In Josh's arms, she became a new woman, one who was comfortable with herself and beautiful.

Another meteoroid raced across the sky. *I wish this date could last forever.*

He pressed his lips against the back of her head then kissed down her neck. She leaned back further, enjoying his touch, longing to feel him inside her once more. Or maybe for a lifetime.

His hands slid under her shirt, caressing her sides, then moved up to her breasts. Each gentle stroke from his thumbs across her nipples sent her senses soaring.

"I want to taste you," he whispered. "Every inch of your amazing body."

She closed her eyes and breathed in the crisp mountain air, along with his sexy, masculine scent. She turned to face him, forcing him back onto his elbows. "Not before I taste you." His erection had already made its presence known against her back, but now it strained against the fabric separating their bodies.

She slid down his legs, taking his sweat pants with her. His exposed cock stood rigid before her, beckoning her hands and mouth. *Such perfection.*

He sucked in a breath as she took his engorged flesh into her mouth. She swirled her tongue around the tip, tasting his arousal. Up and down, taking more in each time, she reveled in the pleasure she found with each moan that escaped him. She had never wanted to please anyone more. As she raked her teeth along his length, he bucked underneath her.

Sitting up, he grasped her shoulders, removing her mouth from him. "God, Tamara, you drive me to the edge of sanity." He swung her around until she lay on the mat, and he hovered over her. "It's my turn."

He slid off her pants then laid kisses across her face, down her body, and in her most intimate places. Traveling further down, his tongue grazed her inner thighs. If he continued, he would make her come long before he entered her.

At the end of the mat, he lifted her foot toward him. She pulled it back, but he held on and used his tongue to numb her mind and heighten each sensation. She'd never felt more loved.

She froze. *No, not love. Love is not allowed on a one-night stand.* How could she even think that word? Lust, sure, but to admit even that would make the morning that much harder.

"Um, Tamara, are you still with me?" He held her foot in his hands, his thumbs rubbing against the sole.

"Yeah, that just feels really good." She would never reveal her thoughts to him.

"I'm glad, because I'm far from finished. Turn over."

She shifted onto her stomach. *What else does he have planned?*

All her tension left as he ran his hands up the backs of her legs to her buttocks. When his tongue met the line where her legs joined the rest of her body, she came close to melting into the sleeping bag. He didn't stop.

"Josh, just fuck me now. I want you deep inside me." She couldn't take any more torture, couldn't handle the intimacy making her long for more once the night ended.

"Not until I'm done." The growl in his voice left her stomach fluttering. She'd never had any man spend so much time on her body, even when she'd had hair on her head.

He lifted her hips, bringing her up onto her knees then positioned himself behind her. She sucked in a breath as his tongue traveled through her swollen folds. How much longer did he plan on teasing her?

He lapped at the dampness between her legs over and over, leading her into oblivion. Intense pleasure built within her. A finger slid inside, then two, gliding in and out, bringing her even closer to release.

"I'm going to make you come now." His thumb only grazed her clitoris and she burst in ecstasy. Lights danced before her eyes. She heard each pop, although the fireworks existed only in her mind.

"That's it, that's how I like it." Removing his fingers, he broke their connection.

She rolled over onto her back, enjoying the waves of pleasure still coursing through her body. Reaching between her thighs, she touched her moist, swollen flesh. She needed to be touched there, needed to be filled again. He'd only made her want more. When his finger grazed the top of her hand, she pulled it away from her core.

"Don't stop on my account." He guided her hand back to her heat. "I think that is so fuckin' sexy. I want to feel you touch yourself. I want you to make yourself come."

She'd never been nervous to masturbate until now. How could she concentrate with him watching? She'd normally picture some hot guy, but...she had him sitting right beside her. She didn't have to imagine anything.

His hand encouraged hers to explore. She watched his eyes widen as she circled her fingers around and into her sweet spot. He did a much better job, but the feeling was more enjoyable than masturbating by herself. His hand continued to feel her every movement while he stroked himself. The wave came quickly, taking her over. He planted her fingers inside, heightening her release.

"Fuck, that was amazing to watch, but now it's my turn."

She heard the tear of the foil wrapper before he lay down beside her.

"You're so beautiful, Tamara. Promise me you'll never forget that."

He made her feel beautiful, but the next time she looked at her bald head in the mirror, she'd forget his whispered words.

"Promise me."

She couldn't, but his lips brushed down on hers, taking away her ability to speak. His fingers met her aching core as he settled between her legs, and he lifted her hips, resting the tip of his hard cock against her pussy.

"Oh," she cried as he drove into her. With each thrust, she arched up to meet him, sweet ripples of pleasure filling her body. As she neared another glorious release, his movement became erratic.

His face clenched and with one final stroke, he led them both to an explosive climax.

Why did Madame Evangeline have to be so good at finding perfect matches? Now, he had an amazing woman cradled into his body and he never wanted to let her go. How could he convince her to see him again, with his unpredictable and crazy life? She didn't deserve what the media would throw at her if she dated him, but he wasn't willing to let her walk away.

He pulled her even closer to him. "Tamara?"

"Hmm?" The sound came out like a purr, exciting him all over again.

"I have a confession to make."

She turned to face him, her eyes wide and waiting.

Maybe this wasn't the best way to convince her to be with him, but he needed her to know. "When I walked into the hotel room tonight, I had no intention of spending the night with anyone. I just wanted some time by myself, away from everyone."

She tried to move further away, but he wouldn't let her.

"I've had many girlfriends before the accident; I won't lie. But they've all been with me because of what my money and status could do for them. And after the incident and the surgeries.... I'd given up on finding someone who actually wanted to be with me."

Fuck, now he was getting all emotional. He had to gain control before she thought less of him. "Anyway, when I went out into the hall, I received a text from Madame Evangeline. She told me that my brother had an arrangement with her and that you were my date for the evening."

He took a deep breath then kissed her forehead. "I didn't think I wanted a girlfriend in my life right now." He pulled her closer. "But I think you're exactly what I've been looking for."

Her bottom lip trembled. A tear fell down her cheek and he wiped it away.

"Talk to me, Tamara. I need to know how you feel because I don't want this to end. I want to take you out for dinner tomorrow, or I guess, tonight. I want to see where this goes, but I need to know how you feel. No matter where I go, I'm going to be followed, but I want them to see you by my side." He waited for her response, but she only stared at him. "Tamara, tell me what you're thinking."

"I...I have to go back to Ottawa next month."

Was she only using that as an excuse? He refused to beg, to act desperate, but would he ever find another woman like her again? "You're still here for another few weeks. I'm sure I could find some time in my busy schedule to spend a few hours with you now and again, maybe every night. That is, if you're willing to be chased by the paparazzi wanting a picture of the hunk you're spending time with."

She punched him in the arm then smiled when he feigned pain. "A bit cocky, aren't we?" The twinkle in her eyes shone more brilliant than the stars shooting across the sky.

"C'mon. I saw the way you eyed my house. You know you want to see the inside, but you won't be able to if you don't agree to go out with me again."

She drew in a deep breath. "Oh, I don't know. That's like a huge commitment to be the girlfriend of Josh Summers, superstar."

Running a hand up her side, he stopped at her breasts, caressing them until she purred again. "There are some benefits to being my girlfriend." His fingers traveled down her stomach to meet her moist core. Ready to take her over again, he slid his finger inside of her.

She arched up to take him deeper. "Oh, Josh, don't tease me this time."

He pulled his finger out. "I'm not really looking for a one-night stand anymore. I prefer to have sex with my girlfriend, and I'm hoping that's you."

"Is that your way of asking me out?"

He adored her playful nature; she complemented him so well. "Yes."

"Then yes, I will be your girlfriend. Now, make love to me."

He couldn't get the condom on fast enough. He entered her molten core, and she pulled him down on top of her.

He didn't take long to reach his release. As he shot his load, she found her own climax, writhing beneath him.

Lying beside her once more, he brushed the sweat from her forehead.

"Well, I'm glad you decided to come back into the room

tonight." Her satisfied gaze continued to stir long forgotten emotions.

Somehow, the magical Evangeline had found his perfect match. Pulling her in closer, he looked up at the sky, watching the meteor shower. "I am, too."

Celestial Seduction

Chapter One

"What do you mean, you want to stay?"

Frey balled his fists and watched the Mission Commander's face turn from blue to purple to red. But he refused to step onto the ship. "Exactly that. I don't want to return to Ginnun. I've spent one rotation around the sun here, established myself in their culture, and lived like one of them. And I'll continue to do so. This is my home now."

"One rotation is hardly long enough to call this place home. Besides, you've sworn your life to the Space Service." As his MC's eyes hardened further, Frey noticed all the wrinkles in the man's once again blue face. His white hair stood up straight on an oversized head. If he remained with the Space Service, the stress of the job would age him exactly the same way.

"This is my last mission. I'll be discharged when I return." Frey wouldn't receive any compensation for this mission, but Space Service credits were of no use on Earth.

"The only way to get out of the Service is to apply for mating. Won't Tandee be waiting for your return?"

His stomach clenched upon hearing her name. "On the day we left, she confessed to already mating with Brand, my supposed best friend."

The Commander only raised his eyebrow. Frey didn't expect any compassion from him. "Ouch! So that's why you failed to keep your emotions in check on the trip to Earth."

He looked away. Even after his time on this planet, the memory of that day still stung. She'd flaunted her admission without a hint of regret.

"There are many other females on Ginnun who would take you as a mate."

Frey looked back to the Mission Commander and shook his head. "I don't want an emotionless relationship. When I choose a mate, I need to *want* to be with her. I want a mate for more than just procreation. I want to love."

"Emotions just get in the way of your life." His MC slammed his fist against the ship. "You're our best field informant! If you're leaving the Service, you could easily find yourself on the High Council. You don't want to throw away your future for the overly sensitive women here on Earth."

"It's not just the women. I have friends here, not just acquaintances, as everyone is to me on Ginnun." Many people he'd trusted on Ginnun wound up stabbing him in the back, as in his best friend who slept with his intended without any guilt. Returning to a planet of long-dead emotions held no appeal after living on Earth. He refused to hide his feelings again, and there were so many more he wanted to experience.

The Mission Commander signaled to the pilot to start the engines. "Stop this nonsense and get on the ship."

"No." He grabbed his sack and without remorse, turned his back on his Ginnunian heritage.

Chapter Two

Carrie searched the hotel bar one more time. After two hours, she had to assume her date stood her up. Heck, it wasn't even a date. The arrangement with Madame Eve only included a one-night stand with no guarantees for anything afterward.

She left the bar. *God, why did I agree to this? Am I that desperate?*

The truth? *Yes.*

But her first date after her divorce failed, as did her marriage.

She'd married her high school sweetheart. When he left her, her heart shattered. It was bad enough to be told she could never have children, but when Peter asked for a divorce three years ago, her life crumbled. Learning of his remarriage and pregnant wife led Carrie to desperation. With no real dating experience, the only night she did go bar-hopping with friends, she heard the word *cougar* whispered over and over and she vowed never to go again. As a pediatric nurse, she didn't have much opportunity to meet many available guys anyway. Her options were limited.

The night she found out her ex-husband had become a father, her best friend, Tamara, had come over to share a tub of Ben & Jerry's Magic Brownies ice cream. "Carrie, you really need to go out and have some fun. Stop moping around." She pointed her spoon at her. "Now, I'm going to set you up on a date. It's through a very popular dating service that so many of my friends highly recommend. The owner, Madame Eve, thoroughly screens everyone before matching them up. Leah married her match a few months ago."

Tamara helped her fill out all of the online forms, but she locked herself in the bathroom to write the letter as to why she wanted to use the dating service. Terrified with thoughts of what Tamara would have told Madame Eve if she waited, she hit send. It couldn't do any harm to apply.

Two months later, she received an email revealing her perfect *1Night Stand.*

"One-night stand?" she asked Tamara over the phone. "I thought I applied to a dating service, not a sex hookup."

"Calm down, Care. It *is* a dating service. You're guaranteed one night of fun, something you desperately need."

"But, am I expected to have sex on the first date?" Before even agreeing to the date, her stomach twisted in knots. "I don't think I can do that."

"Yes! You're wound up so tight, you need a good lay, but of course no one will make you do anything you don't want to." Static crackled over the phone. Had she lost reception? "Hold up, I'm coming over to help you arrange this."

Before she could object, Tamara hung up.

She thought about sending a reject message back, but when she took a closer look at the profile on her computer, she decided to wait for Tamara.

Six foot one, her date owned a successful construction company, and the picture....he resembled every man she'd ever fantasized about. His dark brown, wavy hair looked perfect to run her fingers through and his eyes...*bedroom* didn't even begin to describe how enticing they were. She got wet just looking at them in a picture. Oh, she needed to see them up close.

"God, he's gorgeous," Tamara said.

Carrie blinked. Since it took Tamara twenty minutes to get from her place to Carrie's, she'd been staring at the picture all that time. She flushed, trying to shut her laptop, but Tamara held it open.

"Not so fast. I want deets. What's his name? What does he do?"

"His name is Frey; weird, but I can live with it." She read his impressive profile to Tamara.

"Wow, Madame Eve certainly worked her magic here. He's perfect for you." Tamara crossed her arms and pouted. "I only wish my match had been as perfect for me."

"You used this dating service? Why didn't you tell me?" She would have been less reluctant if Tamara had revealed that earlier.

"Because I didn't want my experience to stop you from letting Madame Eve find your perfect match."

"She didn't find yours?"

"I thought she did. I mean, Josh and I enjoyed our first date and we kept seeing each other afterward, but two months later, we went our separate ways for work. Now dating is so much easier for me. You've seen how my self-confidence has improved."

She *had* noticed the change in Tamara. "Yeah, I guess." *Can I really do this*? She didn't plan on playing the field like her best friend though. Carrie wanted to find her true love.

Clasping her shoulder, Tamara interrupted her thoughts. "So, let's arrange this date. Perhaps you'll meet your future husband or just have a good lay to get you out of the house and improve your mood."

"Tamara!"

Her friend laughed as she sat down at the computer.

Chapter Three

After emails back and forth between Frey, Madame Eve and Carrie, they finally agreed to have the date at a Castillo Resort in Ottawa. Carrie would have preferred to meet at a coffee shop. Being alone with a strange man in a hotel room made her nervous, but she would have the room all to herself now since he hadn't shown.

Frustrated, she took the stairs to the luxury suite, rather than the elevator, trying to delay the loneliness as she walked into the room.

Moving past the foyer, any feelings of dejection fled as she stared at the king-size bed, fireplace and whirlpool tub. Even without a hot date, she could enjoy staying in this room. She planned to have a long soak in the tub sitting in the corner of the room followed by a good night of sleep in a bed not previously shared with her ex-husband.

While the water ran, she stripped and searched her overnight bag for something to sleep in. Tamara insisted on packing the bag that morning and included some black lacey getup meant to cover her boobs and crotch, but there wasn't enough material to cover anything. It didn't matter. She wouldn't be wearing it anyway.

Disappointment clutched at her stomach. Her first date since high school and she'd been stood up. Maybe the man of her wildest fantasies thought her nothing more than the girl next door.

God! I have to stop thinking like this before I spend the night dwelling on this failed date and my failed marriage. No, I'm going to enjoy myself. She gave up on the search for clothes to wear to bed. Then she poured a glass of complimentary wine she'd found in the kitchenette and placed it on the side of the tub along with a bowl of strawberries from the fridge. She slid into the tub, turned off the water and switched the jets on. Total relaxation.

Chapter Four

"Frey, I insist you return at once."

He fixed on his former Mission Commander's fierce eyes. "You had to abduct me to say this? Even after two years, the answer is still no."

"If I leave now, you will have no choice."

He heard the threat in the older Ginnunian words and reigned in his anger. "And if you do, I will hijack the ship and return to Earth. You know I can do it."

"But the Chancellor...."

"....can kiss my ass." All control slid away. The MC found his sore spot. "The Chancellor's daughter left me first. I don't care if Brand died and now he has no one to give him an heir. Tandee can find someone else to fuck her."

His former MC flinched. "You do not belong here. You can do things the people on Earth can't. You don't even look like them. This human image that you're hiding under is just that—an image." His face became red. "You're not one of them. Take it off! If they find out...."

"They won't. This is where I belong, now let me off this ship." Frey didn't once regret his decision to stay on Earth. He'd had enough of the ship, his former Commander and the conversation. With more pressing matters, he needed to leave. "I'm late for a meeting."

The MC's eyes narrowed. "What kind of meeting?"

For a second, he hesitated. "A date." That kind of fraternization was expressly forbidden by the Space Service, but they no longer held any control over him.

The MC stumbled backward. He pushed a hand against the wall to regain his balance. "You've chosen an Earthling as a mate?" He clearly understood the implication.

"I have." He'd yet to meet the woman, but the picture he'd seen of her caused his heart to thump faster, his blood to flow to places only used in mating. He examined the ship for possible exits so he could get to her.

The ship lurched as it dropped in elevation. Within minutes it landed and the ramp door opened.

"Get out!" His former Mission Commander all but shoved him out of the ship. "You don't deserve Tandee. I will inform the Chancellor you are dead."

Although the old Ginnunian meant his words to hurt, Frey smiled as he stepped off the ramp. Staring across the recently harvested cornfield, he spotted his car parked on the side of the road. He rushed across the frosted dirt and corn stalks toward it, with the light reflected from the moon illuminating his path. He'd finally ensured no one from Ginnun would return for him.

Chapter Five

The door handle to the hotel room rattled. Carrie stopped reading and waited. She hadn't ordered room service; they would knock anyway.

She shot upright as Frey, the man she recognized from his profile, burst into the room. "Sorry I'm late. I would have called you, but I couldn't get any reception." With eyes wide, he stared at her, a slight grin on his lips as she stood naked in front of him. She threw towels from the edge of the tub at him. "Turn around!" Trying to cover herself with her hands, warmth spread from her cheeks to her ears and down her neck.

He turned around and picked up something from the floor. As he sidestepped toward her, she cringed. "I'm just going to hand you a bathrobe. You might be more comfortable wearing that for now."

For now? Yes, the one-night stand. Nerves attacked once again. Taking the robe, she wrapped it tightly around her body. He held out his hand to help her out of the tub, but she only stared at him. This man who'd left her waiting for hours wanted the date to go on? No apologies? Then she met his eyes, reminding her of tropical waters and captivating her very soul. She reached for him without any conscious thought.

"Why don't we sit by the fireplace?" He led her to one of the loveseats in front of it.

She wanted to yell at him, put him in his place for disrespecting her, for stripping away more of her self-confidence, but she couldn't form the words. Her heart pounded. *He's even better looking in person.* With her hand held firmly in his, anger ebbed away with each step. Maybe the night would turn out better than she'd expected, so long as he didn't disappoint her again. One night in the presence of this god-like man couldn't hurt.

She wanted to see every inch of him, to burn his image in her mind for the nights she decided to satisfy herself. She might regret it in the morning, but she held no desire to let him out of her sight that evening.

She expected him to sit beside her and whisper sweet nothings before he became familiar with her body. He sat on the loveseat across from her instead. That gesture snapped her out of her trance, and made her more comfortable. Maybe her instincts held some merit. She *could* spend the night with the captivating man.

"You are very beautiful, exactly what I hoped for when I applied to Madame Evangeline's service."

"Thank you." Blushing, she stopped herself from telling him he was drop-dead gorgeous, that she suddenly didn't care if the date only lasted one night. But she couldn't say anything else, her ability to speak vanishing. His eyes captivated her, their greenish-blue color blending into his pupils and she couldn't stop staring.

"So, how long did you have to wait before Madame Evangeline found your perfect match?"

"I...."

He laughed, the sound deep yet gentle. "You know, I'm just as nervous as you. I worried that you'd leave without meeting me. I'm really sorry for being so late."

She hadn't wanted to go home. It would only remind her of another failed relationship.

He continued, "I had to wait six months to find my perfect match."

Six months? She couldn't imagine looking for a date that long. Not looking at all became much easier. She focused back on him and found her voice, too curious not to say anything. "Why so long?"

"Let's just say I have very particular tastes. Don't worry, it's nothing kinky, but I require a partner who is....open-minded."

She didn't know how open-minded she was since the idea of a one-night stand made her panic and the thought of leather and chains made her cringe. *I'm so inexperienced. Maybe I should have followed Tamara's advice long ago and stepped outside of my comfort zone.* But, she arranged the date and would try to remain as *open-minded* as possible.

"I read on your profile that you are divorced." His voice sounded so soft, gentle. He didn't make her feel like a failure. "Will you tell me what happened to your marriage?"

He caught her by surprise. She found it hard to focus on anything in his presence. "I....wow, you sure are forward."

"I really want to know as much as I can about you."

Does he really care that much? "It's going to take more than one night to get to know me."

He left the loveseat and sat down next to her, placing his hand on her thigh. "I understand, but we're here now." He brushed a thumb across her lips.

She could only sigh, craving his attention more than anything.

"Will you please tell me?" he asked. "My....fiancé left me for my roommate. I understand the hurt of a broken relationship."

She looked into his eyes, wanting to tell him her entire life's story with the compassion he showed her.

"I can't have children. My ex-husband left me to be with someone who could. We could have adopted, but...."

He wrapped an arm around her shoulders. "Shhh, don't tell me any more. I see this topic causes you pain, but from what I understand from your profile, you are a pediatric nurse. How are you able to cope every day, caring for children, but knowing you can't have your own?"

"I guess it's my way of dealing with it. With such long hours, the hospital feels less like my workplace and more like my home. But it's always felt that way, even before I knew I couldn't conceive a child." She'd never really thought of her life that way, but it had become her reality. She'd go back to her apartment to sleep and shower, but could never forget about all the children she'd return to on her next shift.

"If you found a way to have your own child, would you still want to?"

With his arm around her, she wanted to lie back against his chest. It felt so intimate, so comforting, but her guard lingered. She'd only just met him. "I can't think like that anymore. I've come to the conclusion I'll never give birth to a child of my own, but I haven't ruled out adopting in the future."

He pulled her closer, her side pressed against his. "I appreciate you answering such personal questions. Now, ask me anything. It's only fair you know more about me. I don't want you to think of me as a stranger."

Carrie pulled away. No matter how hard she tried not to think about it, Frey would never be more than a stranger, one she went there to have sex with. Asking a couple of questions about him would not change that for her. "I....I don't think I can do this." She stood, rushed to the bathroom and locked the door. Hoping he would fulfill all of her fantasies, she still wanted to have sex with him. But not on the first date. Her heart hadn't fully mended. She needed more. As she sat on the toilet seat, the tears flowed. Why did she think she could handle this? She wasn't Tamara. She needed more than just sex. Peter hurt her too much to give herself to someone so freely. She couldn't separate sex from a relationship. Tamara should have gone on the date instead of her. Her friend could easily walk away in the morning.

He knocked on the door. "Carrie, are you okay?"

"I'm sorry Frey, but I can't have sex with you. Your perfect match didn't work out."

"Sex? You think this is just about sex?"

"Yes, that's what we signed up for." She wiped away the tears. "That's what this date was about, the date you showed up three hours late for."

"I said I'm sorry. I had a meeting that ran late. When I tried to call, I couldn't get any reception."

"And I'm sure this meeting was in the middle of nowhere?" She only heard lame excuses from men. Her ex had given her enough when he'd presented her with divorce papers.

"The meeting took place on a private plane and we literally landed in an airport in the middle of farmland. By the time I had any reception, I was only five minutes away."

Her eyes narrowed. She didn't know whether to believe him. "You have meetings with your clients on private jets? What kind of construction company do you run?"

"This was a first. Now, would you please come out and ask questions on this side of the door? Besides, I really need to use the bathroom."

She would have to leave the room eventually since her clothes were still out there. So was the door out of the hotel room.

She opened the door and rushed past him, using the short amount of time he spent in the bathroom to put on as much clothing as possible. Unfortunately, she couldn't find her bra and only managed to get her underwear and camisole on.

He came out and grabbed the rest of her clothes and her overnight bag, a playful grin on his face. "I'll give these back as long as you promise to spend the night here with me. We don't have to have sex, I'll even sleep on the floor, but I don't want you to leave."

She chewed on her lip. Could she truly agree to stay with this gorgeous stranger for the rest of the night and into the morning? If she'd experienced any bad vibes from him, she wouldn't agree to stay. She still worried about having sex. Tamara told her about so many positions and places where she'd done it, but Carrie's ex had only known one way. That's the only way she knew, too. But with the sex out of the way, she could enjoy herself. She'd already paid for the room. "I promise."

He dropped her clothes and bag then reached for her hand. "Let's sit down again. We can order room service because I'm really hungry. The meeting earlier didn't involve any food."

They returned to the loveseats in front of the fireplace and finished off the rest of the bottle of wine. Room service arrived twenty minutes later. For two hours, they ate, talked and laughed, getting to know each other until he no longer felt like a stranger to her. Sadness washed over her when she realized they would only spend a few more hours together before going their separate ways, never to see each other again.

"What's the matter?" Frey asked.

"Nothing, I'm just feeling tired." She refused to dwell on their upcoming departure. She'd signed up for the date with many opportunities to back out. She would enjoy the rest of their time together.

"If you'd like to go to sleep, feel free. I'll just rest right here."

"No, I can't do that to you. The loveseat's not big enough for you to lie comfortably."

"Perhaps we could share the bed. I'm sure there is enough room for both of us without any pressure."

Carrie laughed. The entire night blanketed her with pressure, pressure to sleep with the gorgeous man before her then leave him in the morning, no strings attached. Besides, she didn't think she could *rest* with his body so close to hers. "I may be tired, but I don't think I can sleep."

"Then will you let me do something for you? Will you trust me?"

Trust him? "I....It depends what you want me to do." All of the earlier anxiety came rushing back.

"I want you to lie down. Don't worry, this is nothing sexual and I will not cause you any pain."

His eyes pleaded for her to trust him. She wanted to, she really did. He'd done nothing yet to make her think he would hurt her. "And what are you going to do?"

He smiled a kind, compassionate, understanding smile, one she would enjoy seeing in the morning when she woke up. "Lie down and I'll show you."

She left the loveseat and stood at the side of the bed.

Frey waited for her to get settled before he approached her. "Now I want you to lower your panties."

"Take them off? I thought you said this wasn't sexual." Her anxiety returned and she considered jumping off the bed and locking herself in the bathroom again.

He kept his distance from her, the only thing that kept her from freaking out. "No, don't take them off. Just lower them further down your belly." His voice deepened to a warm and seductive tone and suddenly, she wanted his intentions to be sexual. Lowering her panties, she considered taking them all the way off.

"Not right now." He placed his hand on hers before she could lift her hips to follow through.

Chapter Six

Frey wanted those panties to come off. She ignited something primal inside of him that no other female from Earth or Ginnun could ever spark. But he had to perform the procedure first. It remained the key reason he'd chosen Carrie from all the profiles Madame Evangeline e-mailed him on a regular basis. Evangeline seemed magical in her communications, leading him to almost reveal his secret to her with the hopes of finding the right woman faster. Had Carrie's profile not come his way, he might have. But with her solid frame and lusty curves, he knew she would be able to handle his true alien body. If the date went well, he would reveal his Ginnunian form to her. Seeing her lie there confirmed she wouldn't disappear underneath him. He'd also found some of the confidence he assumed she'd let slip away after her marriage ended. He would bring it back out, make her realize her worth and provide her with a gift no one else could.

"Lie still. This won't hurt, but you will feel warmth from my hands."

She looked unsure, but not scared as he placed his hands below her belly button. "Just relax."

Her eyes closed. "I can't believe I trust you this much. I can't believe I even agreed to this date, but your eyes....they're just so enticing, yet they make me feel calm. Are they contacts?"

He smiled. "I assure you, my eyes are not enhanced in any way and I have no need for contacts." Looking down at her belly, he watched the blue glow spread underneath his touch. Healing transferred through his hands and into her. He filled with immense pleasure at the ability to give her the gift. Even if he never saw her after that night, he would enjoy knowing he'd given her something to bring her happiness.

She opened her eyes and rose up on her elbows. "That feels really weird. What are you doing?"

Whipping his leg across hers, he prepared for her reaction.

Her eyes widened when she noticed the blue glow. She struggled underneath him trying to roll him off. "Get off of me!"

Her hands pounded against his chest, but he grabbed them and held her down with his body. "I'm not hurting you. I'm just trying to help. Will you let me continue?"

Her head shook wildly, her words coming out as a threat rather than in fear. "Get off!"

Her intensity excited him, but he needed to find a way to keep her calm. She refused to look into his eyes. His mouth crashed down on hers, absorbing her next words. She objected at first, but then her tongue reached out to him, a passionate gesture unheard of on Ginnun.

He matched the force of her kiss and skimmed his hands down her arms to rest on her sides near her breasts. She no longer struggled. Her arms wrapped around him, keeping him close. When she released his mouth to take a breath, he sat up. She panted underneath him.

"That was incredible. I....I felt like I was flying through space. So many colors and the brightest stars."

He experienced something different. With that kiss, he had finally found someone who could keep him grounded on Earth and repress any regret for not returning to Ginnun. He brushed his thumb along her cheekbone. "I'd like to continue if you'll let me." He leaned down and placed light kisses across her face.

A sigh escaped her lips and the last of her tight muscles relaxed underneath him. He slid his body down her legs, his hands returning to her belly.

"I thought you were going to continue something else," she whispered.

His cock pressed against his pants already. Her sudden interest in sex made it painful. "I want to, but I need to finish giving you this gift."

Her body moved but she didn't struggle or try to get away. "What exactly are you doing to me? What is this gift? Why was my stomach glowing?"

He took in a deep breath and released it a little faster and louder than he'd wanted. He knew the answer would lead to more questions. While prepared to answer them, he didn't want to scare her away. His response required carefully chosen words to ensure he gave her the gift before he told her of his origins.

"I'm healing you." The blue glow returned across her belly as his hands warmed. "You'll be able to have a child when I am finished."

Her eyes widened. He sensed her fear, but she didn't move. "Your child?"

"No, I am not giving you a child. That can only be done in the usual ways. I am simply making your body able to become pregnant and carry a child."

Carrie propped herself up on her elbows. She stared down at her belly, but remained calm. "How? No doctor could do that for me. How can you? Are you some type of voodoo priest or something?"

"No." He needed to continue and keep his heritage from her for as long as possible.

"A religious fanatic who thinks I'm possessed by demons?"

Frey laughed. "Nope." He was almost finished. Just a little longer. The scarring had all returned to normal, healthy tissue. He only needed to stimulate the maturation and release of eggs in her ovaries.

"How then? I know you're doing something to me. I can feel it."

"Remember how I said I needed an open-minded partner?"

She nodded, her eyes catching a quick glance from his before returning to her stomach.

Just a couple more minutes and he'd be finished. He prepared to hold her down should she freak out when he told her he came from space. "I'm not exactly like you and most of the people on Earth. I'm....different."

"Like a demon or a guardian angel?"

He laughed. It sounded forced, but he needed to stay focused on healing Carrie rather than mating with her. "No, you're thinking paranormal. Try science fiction."

She began to squirm under him, but he didn't need to restrain her. "A....clone? Artificial intelligence?"

He finished healing her and lay down beside her. His thumb ran across her lips, wanting to taste them again, but knowing he probably wouldn't. "Try alien."

Her mouth curved into a smile. "Alien. I don't think so. You're missing the big head and eyes, the green skin, the willowy limbs."

He touched his fingertips to the side of her head. "Like this?" He flashed an image of the alien Earthlings always expected to arrive from space.

"Yeah, but how'd you do that?" Fear shone in her eyes.

Leaving the bed, he sat on one of the loveseats. The night was over. In a second, she'd dress as quickly as possible and rush out of the room. "I told you, I'm an alien from outer space." Perhaps he shouldn't have told her. He would spend the rest of the night alone.

Chapter Seven

Her hands flew to her stomach. It still tingled from his touch. Had he told her the truth? Was he really an alien? And could she now have a child?

She'd spent months wishing for some miracle to help her get pregnant, but nothing worked. Doctors pronounced having a child of her own impossible. And now, with the simple touch of his hands, he believed he'd made all of her dreams come true.

She wanted to believe him, too. She brought one hand to her lips. The magical kiss that revealed the unseen beauty of space. And the endless depth of his eyes. But could she believe him?

No, aliens don't exist. Or did they? How else could she explain the blue light from his hands and the resulting sensations she'd felt inside? And how could he do things the doctors could not?

If his words were true, she should run away, get as far away from him as possible before he began experimenting on her. Or had he already? But none of his actions brought her any harm. He'd only held her down and kissed her to keep her calm. And maybe even given her the chance to become a mother.

But oh, that kiss.

And now, he sat on the other side of the room, giving her space and time to think things through.

But he doesn't look like an alien! Why would he make that up though? What would he gain?

"Frey?"

He looked over, his eyes empty, hollow. She'd never seen anyone look as sad without shedding a tear, quite the transformation from the confident human she'd seen enter the room hours earlier.

Guilt overwhelmed her for wanting an answer to the question in her head, but she asked anyway. "Is that what you really look like? I mean, you're like the perfect male specimen."

She hoped he'd respond with a smile, but he just shook his head, eyes cast down. "It's just an illusion created to help us fit in on Earth."

She hid her panic, but her mind raced with thoughts of an alien invasion. "Us? There's more like you?"

"There were more of us, but everyone else returned to Ginnun. I'm the only one left on Earth."

Phew! "Ginnun, what's that?"

"My home planet."

"Oh, but why? Why did you come here and why did you decide to stay?"

He glanced toward her. His eyes no longer held any color, their blackness appearing wet. "We came here to learn. The disguise is to prevent spreading fear and violence with our arrival. We mean no harm, but as my kind has travelled through space over the centuries, we have never been met with peace."

She could understand why. Most people on Earth believed aliens would only come to the planet to take over. Unsure what she believed, she trusted Frey had no intention of hurting her, he'd had plenty of opportunity already. "Again, why did you stay?"

His eyes blinked—sideways. She tried to hide her gasp, but failed and he looked away. "Like I told you, my intended one mated with my former friend. I had no one to return to."

She slid to the end of the bed, wanting to get closer to him. "Don't you have family, friends? Are humans really that interesting?" She walked toward him, curious to know and see more.

"No one that matters." He paused as if he noticed her getting closer. "On Ginnun, we are taught from a young age that displays of emotion are banned, not that those teachings are always successful. Parents aren't supposed to love their children and husbands can't show any affection for their wives. When Tandee gave herself to another, it tore me apart, but I wasn't allowed to feel that way. After only a month here, I knew I didn't want to return to Ginnun. I wanted to *feel*."

She stood in front of him then and held out her hands. His black eyes met hers as he wrapped her hands in his. "You're okay with what I told you?"

"No, but I'm trying to stay open-minded." She tried to keep her hands from shaking even as she showed him she could handle the information. "I don't feel like you want to hurt me though."

He lightly squeezed her hands, a smile forming on his lips. "I would never bring you harm."

Lifting one hand up, she gently placed it on the side of his face. "Will you show me what you really look like? I can see your real eyes, but I want to see the rest."

"You won't run away?" She winced seeing all of the confidence he'd had at the beginning of the night gone, but it made her trust him even more. "Whatever you do, please don't scream."

"I promised to stay the entire night, didn't I? And don't worry, I don't scream unless someone sneaks up on me, or if I see a spider. You don't look like a spider, do you?" The very thought sent a chill through her body.

He smiled, some of his confidence back while his human image flickered for a few seconds before completely disappearing. Unsure what to expect, she tried not to judge until she'd set eyes on his entire figure. Long, spindly fingers intertwined with hers. He tried to let go, but she held them tight. His body appeared taller and leaner than before. She saw the same black eyes, a less prominent nose and barely visible ears. His hair became jet black and appeared longer and curlier than before. Underneath luminescent scales, his skin shone a light blue.

"So, what do you think?" His mouth quirked, revealing his

uncertainty.

Except for their color, his lips were the only thing that didn't change. She leaned toward him, wondering if they would still feel the same. She had to stand on the tips of her toes to reach him, but wrapping her arms around his neck helped. The feel of his skin surprised her. Perhaps he didn't have scales, but the pattern lay beneath his skin.

He's beautiful.

His lips were softer, warmer. When Frey responded to her kiss, it produced an urgency inside her that pushed away any lingering fear or hesitation. His hands cradled her ass and lifted her up, closer to him. She wrapped her legs around his waist. "Why don't we get those clothes off and see what the rest of you looks like?"

Chapter Eight

He carried her over to the bed. Frey hadn't expected her to remain so calm after taking in his appearance. And her kiss surprised him and stirred his desire for her once more. She'd been worth every minute he spent waiting.

Before they reached the bed, she had his shirt, already torn open from his change, off his shoulders and began to run her fingers down his chest. "Your body is more ripped than I imagined." Her mouth trailed kisses across his neck and down his chest, readying his body for mating. He'd seen the act performed in the instructional videos, but it did not include touching the way Carrie touched him. The male in the video always took much longer to be ready to mate.

When he set her down, she kneeled in front of him, tugging at his belt. "I want these clothes off."

Her hands were quick. His pants fell to the floor and her hands surrounded his cock before he could worry what she'd think. While his shaft was smooth like a human male's, the head had several nodules that released his mating fluid.

She looked up at him and smiled while her thumb brushed across the bumps on the end of his cock. Tandee had never touched him down there. *When our time for mating arrives, I will prime you,* she'd always said. *Until then, it is an unnecessary action that will make you act in an inappropriate manner.*

Unnecessary or not, his body filled with need. He wanted to plunge himself inside Carrie and release his seed.

His knees buckled as she took his cock into her mouth. About to object and ask her the purpose of the act, he lost all thought, trying hard to keep himself standing. Then he remembered the *human* instructional videos for sex. This happened all the time. He'd never understood why until now.

Her tongue flicked over his nodules as she drew him in and out, sending pulses throughout his body. He couldn't take much more. *I must mate.*

With little pressure, he pushed back on her shoulders. "You have to stop that."

"You didn't like it?" She looked away, her newfound confidence fading. "I'm sorry. I never thought that you wouldn't find the same pleasure as a human."

Frey sat on the bed beside her. He brought her head to rest against his chest. "That felt amazing, but I was ready to release. I had to stop you." He lifted Carrie's chin and met her lips with his.

The sensations rushing through his body convened at his soul. His desire for her overwhelmed his self-conscious thoughts. She accepted him without reservation.

He slipped his hands under her shirt, needing to remove her clothing before they could mate. She lifted her arms then hips, allowing him access to her naked body. He barely managed to stop his hands from reaching out for her breasts. Her smooth skin looked so inviting, but female breasts were off limits on Ginnun, for children to feed from only.

She must have sensed his hesitation. Her body straddled his and she took his hand, lifting it toward her breasts. "It's okay, you can touch them. You can use your mouth, too."

He decided to ignore everything he had learned about mating on Ginnun. Carrie was from Earth. She expected different things. She guided his hands to her breasts then grabbed his cock. Her lips crashed down on his mouth.

He pulled away, gasping for air. "I'm ready; you need to stop that."

She released him and lay back on the bed, the scent of her sex invigorating his senses. On Ginnun, the male would approach the woman from behind, but he wanted to see her face as he made love to her. He wanted the emotional attachment. He slid his body over hers and prepared to mate.

Her muscles tightened and she kept him from entering her. "I'm not ready yet."

He froze, with no idea what to do next. Trying to recall the Earth sex videos for some clue, his mind remained blank.

Taking his hand, she smiled up at him. She held two of his fingers together and guided them towards her heat. A moan escaped between her soft lips as he slid his fingers inside. Her muscles tightened around them as her wetness spread.

Chapter Nine

Carrie's body tensed further as he brought her closer to orgasm. The foreplay started with some reluctance; she suspected sex was simply about breeding on his home planet. He learned fast though and she hadn't been afraid to teach him. His body screamed *sexual god.* She took it as her responsibility to show him what it could do. Sex with an alien never entered her mind before, but she'd never imagined an alien to be so virile. She wanted to experience every inch of him.

He removed his fingers and tasted her, his tongue just as elongated as the rest of his body. She struggled to hold still as it swept around, touching every sensitive spot inside. "I never expected...."

He moved three fingers inside of her, set together like a cock and took her words away.

Finding her clit, he learned that rubbing it drove her wild. "You like that?" She heard all the confidence back in his voice.

As she tried to nod, he plunged his fingers further in. She could only get "uh huh" out as a moan, not wanting to move for fear of losing the sensations. Her moans became higher pitched as he drove into her harder and faster, his thumb rubbing her toward ecstasy. She screamed with pleasure as the orgasm tore through her body.

Frey pulled his fingers out of her and leaned away. "Did I hurt you?"

Her body shook with aftershocks. "No," she panted. "That was....amazing."

He relaxed and brought his hands back to her, his thumb grazing one erect nipple while his mouth sucked in the other.

Without hesitation, he slid inside of her, sending her toward another orgasm. The head of his cock hit her G-spot with every thrust. Pressure continued to build as his mouth came down on hers. *So close.* She couldn't think straight. He grabbed her hips and drove her harder and harder, bringing her new pleasures in so many ways.

A guttural roar filled the room as Frey's body tensed above her. The spray of his seed sent her over the edge once more. She held him inside, enjoying the continuing orgasm, and pulsed around his alien cock.

Collapsing beside her, the sheen of his sweat made his blue skin glow brighter. She curled up beside him and brushed the moisture from his brows. "I never expected to experience anything like that."

He tightened his grip around her. "Yes, I'm glad we arranged this one-night stand."

And there it was—the reminder of the purpose of this night. She'd wanted to forget about the idea of the night of uncommitted sex until she left him. She wanted to remain in his arms for as long as possible, but now she couldn't.

Alien or not, she hoped for something more from him.

He fell asleep, his grip loosening. She used the opportunity to get off the bed and rush to the bathroom. She refused to cry. It would do her no good. Dressing as fast as she could, she kept checking to make sure he remained asleep. Although she would never forget this night, she didn't want to go through the awkward goodbye. It was better that way. She grabbed her overnight bag, slipped out of the room and left her key card at the front desk.

Chapter Ten

The warmth Frey had enjoyed when he fell asleep had disappeared. *Carrie.* Where did she go? His stomach rumbled with hunger. Perhaps she'd gone down to the hotel's restaurant to get something to eat. He would join her after he relieved himself and dressed.

Turning to wash his hands in the sink, he caught sight of himself in the mirror, his true form. He kept his alien body hidden with the human image out of necessity. Even when abducted yesterday, he'd refused to change. But she made him comfortable without his human image. She didn't fear him.

He concentrated to appear human once again; walking around the hotel as a Ginnunian would bring him attention he neither needed nor wanted. Looking for his clothes around the bed, he noticed hers were gone, her bag, her purse, everything. She had left him. He searched the room for a note, something to indicate she would return or contact him, but he came up empty-handed.

He roared in anguish. His only lover abandoned him after their first mating. He sat on the bed, his head in his hands. He should have been worried about her telling his secrets to others, but his heart ached too much. Her rejection hurt far worse than when Tandee selected Brand as her mate.

Perhaps arranging a one-night stand had been a bad idea. Madame Evangeline only guaranteed him one night. But he'd been so sure Carrie would stick around after. They'd bonded on so many levels. She'd only needed a boost of confidence to open up, be herself. And she'd revealed more through their mating than during their entire conversation. Then she left him.

Now, without her, he had nothing. All hope of having a mate and family on Earth vanished, with no chance for him to experience love. He might as well devote his life to the Space Service, but no one from Ginnun would return for him. He was dead to his home planet and destined to live on Earth, forever alone.

Even with another hour before check out, he had to leave the room. Every incredible memory of his night with her brought the realization he would never see her again. He couldn't even email her. All emails came forwarded from Madame Evangeline, stripped of any contact information.

After he finished dressing, he grabbed his key card and headed down to the front desk.

"Did you enjoy your stay, Mr. Berger?" The front desk clerk appeared too chipper for his mood.

"Yes, thank you." As his receipt printed out, a thought occurred to him. "The woman staying with me, what time did she check out?"

"Six a.m., Sir. Said she had an early meeting."

He nodded even though he knew it was a lie. "Thank you." He took his receipt and turned to leave.

"Mr. Berger? Will you be seeing Miss Cooper at all today?"

"I hope to." If only his words were true.

"Could you return her phone to her? She ran out of here so fast and I didn't realize she left it until she was gone."

He couldn't have asked for a better way to get in touch with her. The hotel only had Madame Evangeline's information. "Sure, I'll make sure she gets it."

He rushed to his car with her phone, scrolling through her contact list. Several numbers were listed under work, but he found only two other numbers: her parents and her best friend, the friend who'd encouraged her to go on the date.

He would never tell his own parents about a date, but this was Earth. Would Carrie discuss it with anyone?

Chapter Eleven

Carrie considered going home, but she couldn't be alone. She needed someone to talk to and the only person who would understand was Tamara. Wanting to call to make sure her best friend was home, Carrie discovered she'd lost her cell phone. The thought of returning to the hotel to look for it caused her stomach to twist. Maybe later, when she knew Frey would be gone. She couldn't face him. She refused to say goodbye.

In the foyer of Tamara's building, she buzzed up. "It's Carrie. Are you alone?"

"Yes, just got home from my date. Come on up."

She took the stairs to the second floor, hoping the constant movement would keep her tears at bay. She shouldn't have expected so much out of her one-night stand. When her friend opened the door, the flood gates burst.

"Oh, Care, was it that bad?" Tamara put an arm around her shoulders and guided her into the apartment.

"No, it was great. I didn't want it to end."

Tamara stopped and stared at her like she'd grown another head. "Then why are you here? Why aren't you still on your date?"

She flopped on the couch. "I didn't want to have to say goodbye."

Her friend headed for the kitchen. "I don't get it. If you both had a good time, why couldn't you go out again? Why did you have to say goodbye?" She returned with a tub of ice cream and two spoons.

"Ice cream, this early?"

"Anytime is a good time for ice cream."

Carrie took a spoon. "This is exactly why I came here. You always seem to know what I need."

"Yeah, well I need details." She spooned ice cream into her mouth. "Cough 'em up."

"After we....had sex, he made it clear this was just a one night stand. Then he fell asleep. I took that as my cue to leave. I didn't want things to be awkward when he woke up."

"I'm sorry." Tamara leaned over and hugged her. "I know you were hoping for more, but at least you had a night of great sex."

Carrie nodded, wiping the tears. Everything about their night had been great, until the end.

"So tell me about it. How was he?"

The memory brought a smile to her face. Not just the sex, but their hours of talking, learning of his origins, and his gift to her. *His gift. Can I really get pregnant now?*

Her hands moved to her stomach while Tamara stared at her in anticipation. "It was....cosmic, out of this world." She would never tell Tamara that her date came from another planet. Who would believe her anyway?

"Well, except for the end, I'm glad you enjoyed your date, 'cause mine sucked."

She'd been so wrapped up in her own sorrow, she'd forgotten to ask Tamara about her date. Now she felt like a horrible friend. "I'm sorry, what happened?"

"Don't be. I know you expected much more from the date. Me, not so much."

Carrie looked up at the clock, confused. "If your date was so bad, how come you just got home?"

Tamara's eyes lit up. "I met someone else at the restaurant and spent the night with him."

"You spent the night with a stranger?" She'd done the same thing, but the date happened after weeks of planning. It wasn't on a whim. Then again, Tamara became open to dating outside of her usual type, and had been uninhibited sexually since she'd returned from Las Vegas.

"Not a stranger. Remember my one-night stand I told you about?"

She nodded. Her friend radiated with excitement.

"Well, I was hiding in the bathroom from my date. He kept babbling on about fruit fly mating. The only time he shut up was to check out every other woman in the restaurant. I mean, hello, I've got plenty for him to look at. Anyway, when I finally got up enough courage to return to the table, I left the bathroom and ran right into Josh. He's up here on business. He said that his business meeting was almost over and asked if I wanted to meet up after."

She found a glimmer of hope. She might never see Frey again, but she could get out and date like Tamara, find the right guy and have the family she's always dreamed of. "So what did you do about your date?"

"I paid for my portion of the bill and left him sitting there. Josh met me at the coffee shop down the street an hour later and we went back to his hotel room."

Her friend glowed, the same as she had after sex with Frey. "Will you see him again?"

"I'm not sure, but when I told him I'd be down there next month, he said I could stay with him. And we exchanged our new numbers. I guess that means there's no woman in his life right now."

Her mood brightened due to Tamara's happiness. They sat on the couch and watched reruns of *Firefly* on the sci-fi channel while finishing off the tub of ice cream.

Her eyelids became heavy from a night of no sleep. She stood up. "I'm going home."

"You can crash here," Tamara offered.

Her phone blasted some rock song before Carrie could respond. Her friend grabbed it from the end table and looked at her. "Just wait." She went to the kitchen to talk then stuck her head back out and whispered, "It's Frey."

Her stomach twisted. Why was her date calling Tamara and

how'd he get her number?

"Would you like to talk to her?" Tamara asked him.

When Tamara went back into the kitchen, she assumed the answer was no. *Great! Now my one-night stand is trying to make a date with my best friend.* Maybe he believed Earth girls really were easy. She went to the kitchen to say goodbye to Tamara, but saw her best friend writing on the notepad on her fridge. She swallowed the lump in her throat. They weren't even going behind her back; they were planning a date right in front of her.

Her phone. That must have been how he found Tamara's number. And she had talked up her best friend so much to him, too.

After grabbing her purse from the living room, she rushed toward the door.

Tamara stepped in front of her. "Oh no, you don't. You're not walking out on me like you did to Frey."

"I won't stand around while you arrange a date with my one-night stand." Tears formed, but her anger held them in.

"Oh, Care, I'm sorry that Peter stole so much of your self-confidence that you'd think I would even consider dating someone you'd been with." She wrapped her arms around her. "I would never do that to you."

Carrie wanted to hide under a rock. Had she really said that to her best friend? "I'm so sorry. I was just so disappointed with the way my date ended." No excuse would make up for her accusation.

"Yeah, well Frey was, too. He expected you to be there when he woke up. That's why he wouldn't talk to you; he was afraid you'd hang up on him. He didn't know what he'd done wrong."

She took a step back. Had she misinterpreted everything?

Tamara handed her a piece of paper. "He wants you to stop by his house. You have to go there anyway since he has your phone."

She should make things right with Tamara, but exhaustion overwhelmed her. Too tired to deal with anyone, she wanted to get home to bed before she said something else she'd regret. "What does he want?"

"Besides to give you your phone back? He wants to talk. I get the feeling he was looking for more than a one-night stand, too."

Chapter Twelve

Under his human image, Frey had more confidence yet he could not stop himself from pacing in front of his window. Would Carrie show up and if she did, would she just take her phone and leave him again?

He took a glance around his small bungalow. Her phone sat on the counter dividing his living room from the kitchen. It would give him a chance to invite her in. Nothing else seemed out of place, but he took a quick trip through the house to make sure; sitting still proved impossible.

When he left the bathroom after wiping off the sink for the fifth time, he heard a car pull into his driveway. As she stepped out of her car, he decided to let her ring the doorbell before opening the door. He didn't want to appear too anxious.

"Hi." His throat constricted. Her weak smile did nothing to hide her red, puffy eyes. He'd unintentionally caused her pain and now he needed to make everything better. He wanted to pull her into his arms and absorb all of her pain. Instead he waited for her response.

She stared at her feet. "You have my phone?"

Right to business. Well, he refused to let her go so easily this time. "Yes, come in while I get it for you."

He returned to the foyer with her phone and found her only a few steps inside the doorway. "Carrie, we need to talk about last night."

Tears formed in her eyes. "I'm very grateful for the....gift you gave me. I will always remember you for that, and the wonderful night we spent together."

Unable to hold back any longer, he set the phone down on a side table and pulled her into his arms. He kissed her forehead then trailed kisses down her face to her lips.

She responded briefly before pulling away. "I can't do this."

His heart ripped wide open, but his arms would not let her go. "Why? Are you afraid of what I really am? Does being with an alien disgust you?"

Her expression changed to shock. "No, last night was very special. I have no problems with what you are. I will never forget you."

He lowered his hands to her waist and kept her in front of him. "Then why? Why can't you be with me?"

"I understand why you want to experience other women, but I don't want to be tossed away when you're done. I can't handle that again. It's easier to just leave this now and remember our one-night stand."

Resting his hand under her chin, his thumb brushed across her cheekbone. Her heart was still so fragile after her husband had left her, but he could not let her walk away. "There is a reason I took so long to find my perfect match. It relates to me being an alien, but there's so much more involved."

"Why then?" Even on the verge of tears, her cold words pierced him. "Why should I feel special that you picked me to have sex with?"

He leaned down to kiss her neck then moved his lips to her ear. "Not only did I want to find a gorgeous woman to share my gift with, but I was looking for more than a one-night stand. Ginnunians mate for life."

ঞ

She gasped. Had she heard him correctly? "For life?"

His light kisses on her neck sent thrilling sensations through her body, coming to rest between her legs. She resisted the temptation. She didn't want to go through all that pain again. "Why should I believe you?"

He stood upright. His hands rested on her arms and he held her with his gaze. The black pools of emotion returned. She saw his fear, his desperation.

"I can't make you believe anything, but Carrie, you are my only mate. I never have and never will be with another. If you are not with me, I will live and die alone."

After only one night of staring into his revealing alien eyes, she knew he wasn't lying. They gave everything away. She leaned into his chest and he surrounded her. Her body gave way to exhaustion and her tears flowed. As he kissed them away, she asked, "So what do we do now?"

Will we date? Will we move in together right away?

As if he'd read her mind, his mouth crushed hers, his kiss numbing her thoughts. He scooped her up in his arms. "Let's not worry about the future just yet. You look like you need to sleep." He carried her to his room and laid her down on the bed.

As he lay behind her, molding his body to hers, he changed to his alien form. *This is my Frey now.* His blue, elongated fingers combed lightly through her hair, bringing her a sense of peace. Then he rested his hand on her belly.

She closed her eyes and heard him whisper, "Rest now my love, because in nine months our baby will be born."

Unknown Futures

Chapter One

"Miss Jewel Barnaby?"

Her eyes darted toward the tall, austere man in surprise, nervous tension knotting her shoulders. She almost didn't respond. No one had called her Jewel since she'd left the hospital two years ago. Instead they called her ugly, freak, or monster. The doctors had done all they could, but despite the several surgeries and multiple, painful skin grafts, everyone in Prescott, Ontario would always know her as the girl who was splashed in the face with acid on the biggest night of her teenage life.

They'd been in his garage, grabbing blankets for the after-prom party. When he'd tried to get fresh with her, she'd had to tell him, a jock through and through, she wouldn't sleep with him, that she'd preferred women. But he didn't take no for an answer. Pinned against his truck, her heart racing in panic, she kneed him in the groin. Doubled over, he'd grabbed sulfuric acid from a shelf behind him and splashed it in her face. Everything after that moment became a blur until she woke up in a hospital, groggy with painkillers, a tube stuck down her throat. She couldn't see a thing with the bandages covering her eyes, but felt and heard her mother by her side.

From then on, some of her neighbors looked at her with disgust, sympathy, or fear. Others glanced away when she passed, as if she didn't exist, including her old friends.

The chauffeur simply smiled at her as he reached for her two oversized suitcases. His professional, impassive demeanor calmed some of the butterflies dancing in her stomach.

Standing on the curb, she stared down the road, sure neighbors spied out their windows, wondering why a limo would be picking *her* up. *I need a break from this place.* As she slid over the leather seat of the Ford Excursion limousine, her stomach tightened. Madame Evangeline's text had been brief. *Pack for two weeks. The limo will meet you in front of your building in an hour.* She'd had no time to do anything but change and throw clothes in a suitcase.

Until now. Had applying to 1Night Stand really been a good idea? She could end up with her date running away, screaming. And why had Madame Evangeline told her to pack for two weeks when her date was only supposed to last one night?

She had no one to report to, though, no one who would worry she'd be gone for so long. She didn't have a job. When she handed in applications, she was often told the position had already been filled, and once she'd poked her head back in to ask a question and seen her resume being ripped up before she'd even left the building. All the university courses she took were through distance education. With so much free time, she often kept well ahead of her studies so she had no assignments due for another month.

Her parents wouldn't miss her either; her mother had died a year before from breast cancer. They'd spent so much time together in the hospital. She'd been Jewel's closest friend, her ally, the one person who'd accepted her unconditionally. And now she had no one. Her father only cared about his bimbo of a girlfriend, and made sure to keep the airhead away from his lesbian daughter. Jewel rolled her eyes. She preferred a woman with a brain, not an ass wiggle and an annoying laugh.

In the last two years, though, she hadn't had one date, not even a night out with friends. No one wanted to be seen with her, and after a day of stares at the local college, when she'd gone there to write an exam, she'd returned home and applied to the 1Night Stand dating service. She'd read an account of the wondrous matchmaking abilities of Madame Evangeline on a *Yahoo* group for burn victims. If Josh had found love, why couldn't she?

Jewel had no idea what her date looked like or where she'd meet her. Looks really didn't matter, but she wanted an age, a name, something.... And where was she going? Packing for the Sahara Desert was not the same as packing for the Arctic Circle, so she'd included clothing for both and every climate in between.

When the limo merged onto the highway, she reached into her tote bag for her ereader. Taking her mind off the purpose of her trip might ease her rolling stomach. Throwing up in the luxurious car did not seem like a good idea. She loaded up the most recent book from her favorite science fiction romance series—involving an alien species not as uptight about homosexuality as humans—and became lost in a world more hospitable than her own.

Chapter Two

V stared across the concourse, trying to spot her charges. She'd been told to expect three people through the portal from Earth, two Terran females and a Ginnunian male who might be disguised as a Terran. *How would he look?* The blue-skinned species had never needed to hide their identity on the space station. Would he still show a hint of his natural color, or would he resemble his traveling mates?

They'd all be easy to spot. V was only one of five people from Earth who worked at Space Service Headquarters. Every day, she saw thousands of Phanties, a species with large ears and a trunk like an elephant; Pillites, who reminded her of a giant pill bug; Goopers, blue blobs with eight short tentacles as feet, and many other species from around the universe. But Terrans could only make it out to the space station—perched on the far edge of the Milky Way from their home world—using a portal the government deemed classified.

She'd never dreamed of working off-planet back when she waitressed for a quaint Italian restaurant in New York while putting herself through grad school. But one unusually calm night, she'd served a man who'd reminded her of a character from *Men in Black*. He'd appeared surprised when she'd understood his order—spoken in German.

While her other customers languished, he'd engaged her in friendly conversation. Charmed by his witty repartee, she'd revealed she spoke five different languages and was working two jobs to put herself through school. Along with a generous tip, he'd left his card—containing only his name and number—with *If you're looking for a job that's out of this world, call me* written on the back. Thinking he was some kind of quack, she'd tossed the card in the trash before greeting a new table of customers.

He returned the next night and every evening for a week until she consented to sit down to listen to his job offer. Six months later, after completing rigorous training, she'd walked through the portal to serve as a concierge for the space station's interstellar hotel. She hadn't returned to Earth since then, her position so top secret she'd been unable to so much as tell her boss why she'd quit with no notice. Other than spending a few familiar holidays with her fellow Terrans, she almost never crossed paths with anyone from home.

She continued her education as well, overwhelmed and fascinated by ancient space history consisting of much more information than that of Earth. Still, she missed her own kind. Terrans were seen as inferior to those from other planets, governed by cowards who hid the idea of other life in space, yet took full advantage of the technology. Thankfully, no one held her accountable for Earth's deficiencies.

She was drawn back to the present as the crowd parted in front of her, like the Red Sea to reveal her charges. They walked along with the other new arrivals, oblivious to the multitude of curious looks they received. The blue, lanky Ginnunian male led his very pregnant terran wife toward her. Peering past the pair, V caught a glimpse of a dark-haired woman tucked closely behind them before the crowd closed in once again, grunting, squeaking, and clicking in communication.

She waved to get their attention, thankful her charges had arrived without incident. "Hi, I'm Flavia, but you can call me V. That's what everyone here calls me." Because no member of any other species on the station had been able to pronounce her name without it sounding vulgar in his or her language.

The Ginnunian stepped forward and surprised her by reaching out to shake her hand—not a custom for his people. "Hello, I'm Frey, and this is my wife, Carrie."

She shook his hand and then his wife's, trying to hold in her excitement at meeting someone from home.

Frey moved to the side, revealing the petite woman behind him. "And this is Jewel."

V squealed. Unable to hide her exhilaration any longer, she wrapped her arms around Jewel. Not only was she from Earth, but she looked to be only a couple years younger than her. All the Terrans on-station were her parents' age. For once, her unwavering loneliness would ebb, at least for a few days.

But her hug wasn't returned, only met with a gasp. V stepped back. "I'm sorry, did I hurt you?"

Jewel shook her head, but wouldn't make eye contact.

"I think she's a little self-conscious about her scars," Frey said.

V winced. *Why did he have to mention them?* Sure, she'd noticed, but she had friends with fins, feathers, and elephant ears. A few scars wouldn't stop her from being social. Was that why she'd been asked to entertain Jewel during her stay?

Chapter Three

Jewel tagged along behind the rest. V's hug had taken her completely by surprise. Smiles, now touching? She thought she'd been prepared to go on a one-night stand, to have sex with a strange woman, but maybe she wasn't. Sure, her traveling companions hadn't made her feel like a freak, but Carrie had married, and was now pregnant with, a blue alien. Imagine what Jewel's neighbors would say if they saw Frey on the street.

Leaving the concourse, they traveled down a long hallway. V stopped and placed her hand on a pad beside a metal door, which slid open. "Frey and Carrie, this is your suite. There is a buffet every evening in the dining hall, down the corridor and to your right. If you need anything at all, press the front desk button on the communication panel." She gestured to the screen inside the door. "Enjoy your stay at the SS Hotel, where everyone in the universe is welcome."

Wait! Everyone in the universe? This place is filled with aliens. Jewel's head spun. *Is that why Madame Evangeline sent me here? Because no one on Earth would want to date me?* She cringed. The elephant and the blue women had been somewhat attractive, but she hadn't noticed a difference between the male and female bug people or the blue blobs. Her vision blurred with the onset of tears. *I've made a horrible mistake.*

Something touched her shoulder and she jumped.

"I'm sorry I scared you." V startled her again by reaching to wipe moisture from her cheek. "I wanted to make sure you were okay. I know this place can be overwhelming when you first arrive."

That's for sure. She couldn't imagine living there. "So, will you show me to my room?" She yearned to hole up like she did back on Earth, lose herself in a story until she went on her date with the alien. Except for V and Carrie, she'd seen no other humans on the space station, and she wasn't supposed to meet her date until tomorrow night. Sure, the idea had excited her in her books, but none of the humanoids and other beings she'd seen were fashionista beauties.

She'd gone through a week of emergency procedure training at a top-secret facility even she wasn't allowed to know the location of, with the couple who traveled with her. All of that packing and training for one night with a space creature whom she'd never see again? During that week, they'd met with the director of the space station, an odd character as well; why hadn't she objected then?

V put her arm across her shoulders. "You're staying with me."

"I am?"

"The director thought it might be easier on you, since my suite is set up for people from Earth." She guided Jewel down the hall. "I have an extra bedroom you can use."

"But how's that going to work with my date? Will we go somewhere else?" *Shit!* She wasn't supposed to mention her reason for the trip. 1Night Stand kept their business dealings discreet.

"I'm not aware of the itinerary for your entire stay, but if you have something scheduled, I'll make sure you get there. Right now, I'm supposed to get you settled in and keep you entertained."

V stopped, her arms dropping to her side. "We're about to go in the tube. It's a transportation system for getting around the station. I admit, it feels really weird, but it's the fastest way to my place." She smiled at a giant bug who seemed to have dropped from the sky. It waved a long, skinny limb before skittering off down the hall. "Since you've never traveled this way before, I'm going to hold your hands and we'll go through together."

V pressed a green button on the wall then linked their fingers. Jewel had no time to comprehend how the transport worked before they were sucked up into the air then shot through a narrow cylinder. She now knew what traveling through an industrial vacuum would feel like. If she hadn't been so worried about hitting someone else along the way and how she'd land, she could have enjoyed her proximity to V. No matter how much she tried to deny her feelings, she enjoyed her touch.

When they dropped out of the pipe, V reached out for her, but Jewel wasn't ready for the impact. She crumpled to the ground, pulling the other woman down on top of her.

Giggling, V rolled off. "Thankfully, these floors are padded. I haven't landed like that since my first week here." She jumped to her feet then helped Jewel up.

"I'm sorry. I didn't know what to expect." But she wasn't sorry. Being that close to such a gorgeous woman awakened long dormant desires. *If only she was my date, my one-night stand....*

"No problem. I guess I should have explained the tube before we used it, but we had to get through while it was clear." V grabbed her hand. "Come on, let's get you settled. I have a lot planned."

Planned? That sounded like she wanted to take her out in public. She knew what to expect from people on Earth, but here? She couldn't handle negative reactions from other species. "Um, I'd rather settle in for the night."

"Oh no, I don't think so." V placed her palm on a screen and after a beep, a gray steel door slid open. She pulled her inside. "You can rest for a bit, but I'm taking you to the club tonight."

"A club?" *No way.* She'd refuse to go.

"Yes, like a dance hall back home. The music and drinks are a bit different, but it's the same idea. You should see some of these aliens move."

Her stomach churned. The meal she'd eaten before the day-long trip through the portal wanted to make a quick escape. “I…I don’t think I can go. I need to find the bathroom.”

“You are looking a little green.” V stuck her arm through hers. “Let’s get you to the loo.”

Jewel had no time to take in the apartment. She had to concentrate to keep the food in her stomach.

Chapter Four

V left Jewel in her spare room to rest. The poor woman had so little self-confidence. So what if her face was scarred. She still had the most appealing blue eyes and such soft, creamy skin. Her wavy brown hair would make most women jealous and men want to run their fingers through her locks. She couldn't stop touching the petite beauty. Who on Earth had made her feel so insecure?

Well, I know what I have to do. She would take her out, show her that she didn't have to be afraid to be seen in public, that she truly was a precious gem.

She smiled, thinking of the surprised expression on Jewel's face when they'd been sucked up into the tube. And when they'd landed.... Maybe she should have tried harder to keep her standing, but she'd rather enjoyed landing on top of her. She'd rolled off quickly to keep from kissing her charge. After all, Jewel had traveled there for a date, or so she said. But with whom, and why hadn't the director included that fact in her briefing?

V grabbed the tote full of Earth food, which had come up through the cargo tube with Jewel's luggage. Inside she found pasta, bread, cheese, garlic, red sauce and—*oh yeah!*—strawberries. Her stomach growled already. She hadn't had anything besides replicator food in months, the portal being too expensive to start up for only Terran food.

A beautiful woman and delicious food? Perfect. No! She couldn't have lustful feelings for her charge. She'd make dinner—anything to distract her from slipping into the bedroom and crawling into bed with her houseguest.

It had been so long since she'd been with anyone. Gar, a Phantie she worked with at the hotel, had asked her several times to be one of his bedmates, but she'd turned him down. He didn't understand monogamy. When she chose a partner, whether male or female, she didn't want to share them with anyone else. Gar's current collection of bedmates consisted of five females, each from a different planet.

She started a pot of water boiling for the pasta then opened her last bottle of Canadian Ice Wine and poured herself a glass. She had found a reason to drink it. Now, if only she could figure out a way to get Jewel to the club without making her turn green again.

ଓ

Jewel awoke, the scent of garlic and red sauce making her stomach groan with hunger. *I'm on a space station. How is that possible?* During training, she'd been told to expect tasteless, replicated food. She padded to the adjoining bathroom and returned to dig out a fresh outfit from her luggage. Decorated in silver and blue, V's guest room reminded her of any bedroom back on Earth, with a bed, dresser, closet, and armoire. Unlike the palm activated mechanisms in the public corridor, the door slid open as she approached.

Crossing the plush gray carpeting, she took in the view from the upper landing overlooking the living room, dining room, and kitchen, all open-concept and decorated for comfort and to resemble Earth. None of the floating furniture she'd marveled at in the concourse and hallways of the space station in sight. She followed the winding staircase's graceful curves, amazed that such an elegant fixture would be found on a space station in the middle of nowhere.

V stood in front of the stove, tasting the aromatic red sauce. She'd changed from her drab uniform into black yoga pants and a pink, spaghetti-strap tank top. Jewel could only think of running her hands over the woman's curves, of being underneath her once more.

Waking up to her, to such a domestic scene, felt so normal, so perfect. But it wouldn't last. She'd go on her one-night stand with some alien who could be a creepy bug, return to Earth in a couple of days, and never see the beautiful woman before her again. *Why is life always so unfair?*

V looked up and smiled as Jewel reached the bottom of the stairs. "How are you feeling?" The last time she'd been graced with such warmth was that agonizing day in the hospital when her mother said, "I love you" before succumbing to her cancer.

"I...I'm okay." She had to fight off the memory. She wanted to enjoy as much time with V as possible before she left, even if that meant going out in public. "What are you making? It smells delicious."

"Spaghetti. It sounds like such a simple thing, but I haven't had Earth food in months." V poured a glass of wine then handed the drink to her. "Dinner's almost ready. Come, sit down."

The Space Service had spared no expense in the kitchen, either, furnishing the room with stainless steel appliances and cupboards. Jewel sat on a matching silver hover stool across from V. *I guess she does have floating furniture.*

"This club you were talking about, what's it like?"

Chapter Five

V tapped her fingers with a steady beat on the wall outside the guest room. She couldn't believe Jewel had agreed to go to the club with her. Now she had to wait for her to finish getting ready and she was taking forever.

They'd shared a wonderful dinner, although she'd spent more time watching Jewel savor the meal than enjoying the scrumptious pasta herself. The food and the company made her miss Earth more than ever, but she'd signed a lifetime contract. She'd never set foot on her home planet again.

"Are you ready yet?"

"Almost. I can't decide between the two outfits I brought with my date in mind."

"Pick the one that's the most comfortable." *Or most revealing*. Hopefully the clothes would give a better view of her body. She didn't plan on letting her sit around and look pretty, though. She would get her up on the dance floor and keep her there, letting the music control the rest of their night. And with any luck, Jewel would cancel the date she kept talking about.

Lusting over one of her charges probably wasn't a good idea. She often escorted guests around the space station, but Jewel was the first to stay with her. And she considered it her personal mission to prove to the woman how beautiful she found her.

She gasped as the door slid open.

Jewel emerged, her hair swept up into a loose bun, a few curly tendrils falling down the sides of her face. She wore a purple, lacey camisole, exposing a mouth-watering amount of her soft skin. A black mini-skirt hugged her shapely hips and knee-high black boots gave her added height. Very little makeup adorned her face, leaving her scars exposed. "Do I look okay?" She chewed on her bottom lip.

"Wow! Do you ever." It was all V could do to keep from reaching out to touch her. No, there'd be plenty of time for that later, if all went well. *If she even wants me....*

She considered her own attire—black leggings, long silver shirt, and suede boots. She'd worn the same outfit before and had quite a number of Phanties try to pick her up, but she wasn't after any of them. She wanted the woman in front of her.

Trying to calm her desires, she headed toward the stairs. "Let's get going. The club should be hopping by now."

೧೫

Jewel raced to keep up. The woman moved so much faster than she could, having miles of long, shapely legs. She had to follow her or risk getting lost. When they reached the tube, V hit the button then wrapped her arms around her, hugging her to her trim curves.

She barely registered the suck then push of the tube, trying not to melt in V's arms. Her cheeks flushed and warmth pooled between her thighs. If she remained in her embrace any longer, she'd be useless for the rest of the night. Her jelly legs wouldn't take her anywhere. *Why can't* she *be my date?*

Their landing was much smoother than the first one, with V better able to keep her steady. Then she was no longer in her arms.

"The club's around the corner." V took off again.

The outside walls of the nightspot vibrated in time to the

heavy bass music that pounded out its open doors. Flashing lights shone through the windows and danced across the floor. Inside, floating tables and chairs lined the edges of the room. Her jaw dropped as a tray filled with beverages traveled past her, all on its own. A huge dance floor in the center of the room was crowded with a multitude of species gyrating in ways she could never have dreamed of.

"Music is a universal language. It's probably the one thing Earth has contributed that every species appreciates." V took her by the hand and pulled her toward a bar. "C'mon, let's get a drink."

Assorted creatures stood three deep awaiting service, so Jewel found an empty table and dropped into a seat while V squeezed through the crowd to place their order. A collection of hungry eyes followed V's every move. Some elephant men left a crowd of women to pursue her. Yet, she seemed oblivious to them all. Why? Did she have someone? Had she been with those men already?

How could Jewel ever compete with the exotic figures populating the station? She was plain and damaged. The oddballs filling the dance floor held so much more appeal than her. She blinked back tears of despair. *Maybe I should go.* She'd only hold V back, prevent her from enjoying her night. After all, she had interrupted her hostess's life. She slid off the chair and headed for the exit. *I'll find my way back. Somehow.*

Chapter Six

V grabbed Jewel's arm. "Where do you think you're going?" She'd only been gone for a minute, not even time to get to the bar. *What happened?*

Tears trailed down Jewel's cheeks. "Back to your apartment."

V laughed then covered her mouth. *Shit! She'll probably think I'm making fun of her.* "There's no way you'd make it back on your own. That's why I was asked to escort you around."

"Well, you can *escort* me back to your apartment then."

"Why?" She refused to let Jewel feel sorry for herself. Not here and not with her.

"I see the way everyone looks at you."

Oh no, she knew those games. "Yes, but you didn't see everyone looking at *you*. You didn't *see* the Phantie who followed you out, the one I had to grab and tell to go back inside."

"Really? But I don't want any of them."

V lifted Jewel's chin up and wiped away her tears. "Neither do I."

Jewel only blinked, not seeming to understand her meaning.

V grabbed her hand and pulled her back into the club. If she'd remained where they stood, she would have ended up kissing Jewel. And she couldn't do that. Not when she'd come to the station for a date with someone else. But who? Didn't really matter. She'd still show her a good time, whether Jewel demonstrated any interest in her or not.

"Let's hit the dance floor." The drinks could wait. She wouldn't let her guest out of her sight again.

The music thrummed, filling her to the core, preventing her from standing still. She found a spot with just enough room for the two of them. No one else mattered. With each hit of the bass, she moved her feet, her hips, her hands. She let the beat control her body and her heart.

Although others might be watching, her attention remained on Jewel. Each movement, a planned seduction. She couldn't let her go without trying. When the next song began, Jewel finally relaxed. She moved to the music.

And V moved closer. She slid her hand from Jewel's waist, down, then back up, swaying in front of her. Only an inch between them. She couldn't get enough. Her Earth scent became intoxicating.

Beat after beat, song after song, she kept her hands on the sexy woman. She claimed her, telling everyone else to stay away. She wanted to savor her precious body. Maybe she could make her forget about her date.

She pulled Jewel even closer, her sensitive nipples pressed against the woman she desired. Holding her with both hands, grinding against her to the music. Her heart raced with hunger. *I want to take her on the floor. Right here. Right now.*

But the song changed. The beat slowed, indicating last call. The club would close soon.

Most of the patrons had left. Only those hoping to hook up remained. She stepped back. Jewel would have to make the first move. V could never force herself on anyone.

When Jewel took her hands and placed them back on her body, she couldn't help but smile. Perhaps the evening would end the way she wanted.

Jewel pressed against her, her head resting on her shoulder, swaying to the decelerated beat. "I don't want this night to end."

Their dancing became deliberate, a sensuous and intimate

rhythm. "It doesn't have to."

Jewel stopped and looked up at her. "You...you're interested?"

"Why wouldn't I be? You're the most beautiful creature in the space station." Somehow, she had to make her see. She brushed her thumb across her lips, wanting to touch more, her entire luscious body. Taking a deep breath, V steadied herself. If this were to go any further, Jewel needed to show her own intentions. As warm moisture pooled between her thighs, V schooled herself to patience.

"Are you sure *you're* not my date?"

Shit! That damn date, the only wedge between them. "No, but I wish I was."

"I wish you were, too." Jewel stood on the tips of her toes and claimed her mouth.

V pulled her closer until the bit of space between them had been filled. Excited by the warm, curvaceous body pressed against her taut nipples, she fed from the sweetness of Jewel's mouth, drawing out each delicious sweep. But she wanted more. She wanted all of her.

"Dat so hot!"

The moment expired with the looming presence beside them.

She held Jewel's hand, wanting to maintain their connection, never planning to let her go. She would deal with the situation then finish what Jewel had started. "What do you want, Gar?"

"You, bootiful human and da new one, too." The whites of his eyes glowed red and alcohol-laced sweat coated his gray skin.

"You've had one too many fizzers. Go away. We're not interested."

He pulled out his arousal.

Jewel gasped.

V had heard that Phanties were renowned throughout the universe for their immense cocks, but she had never been curious enough to find out for herself. Looked like the rumors were true.

"You see what you do to me? I want you both for bedmates."

"I said we weren't interested, Gar. Not now, not ever. Put your dick back in your pants before you embarrass yourself further."

She would have it out with him the next time she saw him at work, but for the moment she had other things to focus on.

"What 'bout her?"

Jewel shook her head, squeezing V's hand.

"I watch? Never had two at same time."

"No!" V said.

She giggled when Jewel echoed her response.

"C'mon, let's go." She pulled her out of the club, leaving Gar with his pants around his ankles.

"Wow, he sure was big."

She smiled, relieved Jewel hadn't been horrified by Gar's bad manners...or his gigantic dick. "Yes, a fact that strokes their egos a little too much."

"Have you ever...?"

She cringed. "No. Not exactly my type."

"So what is your type?"

She recognized the fishing. Perhaps Gar had affected Jewel more than she'd originally thought. She stopped walking and took Jewel's other hand, holding them together. "Well, I prefer someone who is beautiful both inside and out." As she tried to look down, V lifted her chin to meet her gaze. "Even if she doesn't realize how beautiful she really is, how precious, just like a jewel."

A tear slid down the woman's cheek, and V wiped it away. "I want you, sweetie." She pulled Jewel against her then reclaimed her trembling, swollen lips. Jewel responded with more passion, stroking her mouth to ecstasy. *We need to get back to my apartment.* She reached over and pressed her palm against the screen for the tube, not breaking contact with her for the entire ride.

Chapter Seven

When they landed, Jewel felt as if she had floated to the floor, like a fairy. She didn't remember any of the trip through the tube, just being in V's arms, tasting her lips, everything. The woman made her believe she was beautiful, that she could find happiness with someone, with V, on a space station. Everything everyone had ever said about her melted from her mind, V's kindness and warmth taking their place.

She pulled away and gasped for air. "We're here already?"

V stroked the side of her face, making her feel precious. "Yes, let's go inside." The door slid open and she pulled her into the foyer. "Would you like something to drink?"

She shook her head. The only thing she wanted was the gorgeous woman in front of her who reminded her what it was like to be a real person again. Not a monster. Not a freak.

"Well, I need a water. I'll be right back."

Waiting, she took another look at the apartment. While the open-concept main level had been decorated in Earth tones, the upper floor resembled the aurora borealis with purples, blues, and greens scattered across the wall by the stairs in a beautiful display. So welcoming, so much like Earth. Yet she didn't feel comfortable enough to wander around on her own. She still remained a guest, only meant to stay for a couple of days.

She took a deep breath as gentle hands swept her hair away from the back of her neck. Light kisses reined across her bare skin, a mouth cold from a drink of water, yet warm with passion.

"I can't stop touching you." V's fingers brushed against her belly. And oh, she wanted more. She wanted her hands on her bare skin, her breasts, over her swollen mound. "Let's go to my room."

That soft voice made her weak in the knees. How would she make it up to the bedroom?

V tapped her butt then walked toward the stairs. "You coming?"

She found the strength and raced her up the stairs, reaching for her, but never quite catching up. Finally arriving on the second floor, she found herself once again wrapped in strong, welcoming arms. "I thought we were going to your room."

"We are, but I couldn't wait to touch you again."

Jewel couldn't wait either. She captured V's mouth, grabbing her by the ass and pulling her hips against hers. Yet she wanted to feel the bare skin underneath the clothes. Without hesitation, she slipped her hands under V's shirt. Touching her soft skin stoked the flames of desire already burning inside. She had to have her. Pulling away from tender, swollen lips, she lifted the shirt off and tugged her own over her head.

Never had she met anyone so perfect, all luscious curves and full, perky breasts. She unclasped V's red, lacey bra, needing her taut nipples in her mouth. Before she could taste her, V grabbed her wrists, raising them above her head.

Backed against the wall, her hands pinned above her head, a knee between her legs—without the support of V's body against hers, Jewel would have melted into a gooey puddle. She tingled with anticipation as if she were a teenager, but then again, she had never dated as an adult.

"Damn, you're amazing." V trailed her fingers down her body. She lifted Jewel's legs around her waist.

Jewel grasped her shoulders for balance.

"Don't worry. I won't drop you." V smiled at her. "And since you're my guest, I get to pleasure you, first."

She wrapped her arms around V's neck. "Then take me now."

V turned and started toward her room, carrying her. "I can't wait."

They arrived at the sliding door, and V set her down. Breathless, she shook off her bra, and V's quick hands hiked her skirt up around her waist. The woman continued her exploration and moved her thong aside to allow her fingers access to her molten core.

"You're going to take me over before we get to your room."

V slid her fingers farther inside. "Is that a challenge?"

Jewel giggled as the door slid open. Unlike the rest of the apartment, this room held no light. Her stomach clenched. Did V leave the lights off so she wouldn't have to look at her scars? She had called her beautiful, but had she meant the words? Maybe Jewel hoped for too much from this woman who wasn't her date.

V lowered her onto the soft sheets. "Give me one minute."

But she curled into a ball. Should she stay there or leave before she allowed herself to have intercourse with someone who couldn't even look at her.

"Candlelight, on. Remove sky screen." With V's words, a multitude of faint lights flickered to life on the walls, causing shadows to dance around the room. Above her, the ceiling slid away, revealing stars through a plate of thick glass.

"There, now I can see you better."

Jewel stretched out on the bed to take in the view above her. She wiped away a tear, hoping the other woman wouldn't notice. *Why do I always assume the worst? I wish I could remain on this space station forever, but I will only be here for two nights.*

V lay down beside her, running her fingers down Jewel's chest, between her breasts, and down to her waistline. "Why don't we get the rest of these clothes off?"

Jewel sat up to take off her boots, then slid down her skirt and thong, leaving them on the floor. V took her time removing her own clothes, baring her perfect body. She could have been a model, probably anything she'd wanted. Why had she given it all up to live in outer space?

V lifted her chin for a long, drugging kiss, pulling her from her thoughts. She straddled Jewel's waist, laying her back onto the bed.

As V captured her nipple between her teeth, Jewel drew in a quick breath, gripping the sheets. It had been so long since anyone paid any attention to her body. Moisture pooled between her thighs.

She raked her fingers through V's blonde tresses, trying to retain some composure, yet not succeeding. Lifting her hips off the bed, she longed for more.

"Mmm, yes, I think another part of you is craving some attention. Let's see how that pussy of yours tastes." V trailed kisses down her stomach, spreading her legs as she traveled lower.

Jewel gasped when a finger passed across her clit. She'd finally found someone who actually wanted to touch her, wanted to make love to her.

As the other woman's tongue ran along her swollen mound, she came undone. Lights burst before her eyes. Each wave of pleasure built upon the one before.

But V kept her head buried between her legs. She lapped up her juices, leading up to another explosive release.

"That's it, sweetie." Moving up to lie beside her, V stroked her face, allowing her time to catch her breath. "You tasted so good."

She wanted to give her the same satisfying release. Flipping over, her wet heat covered V's sex. "It's my turn."

Chapter Eight

V rolled over, a smile on her face before she opened her eyes. Jewel's warm body lay beside her, the beautiful woman still sound asleep. They'd spend hours tangled together, making love.

Her chest ached. She'd known all along Jewel would only be there for a couple of days, she couldn't help her instant attraction or the surge of emotion she felt for her. Now she wanted to return to Earth. But she never could. She'd made the commitment and signed the contract. Her life belonged to the Space Service.

Then there was Jewel's date—why had the director not included that in her briefing? And the Terran's short visit in itself was puzzling—why would she be sent to the station for such a frivolous reason—when V herself had to sign away her life to be there. She couldn't figure out the situation. Didn't want to. She wanted Jewel for herself.

Her stomach clenched. For the first time in years, tears formed in her eyes. *Shit!* Why had she let Jewel into her heart?

She rose from the bed then tiptoed to the bathroom. Maybe a shower would take the ache away. Inside the stall, a cold blast snapped her awake. She should go in to work. *Yes, work.* Jewel would be fine on her own for a few hours. During the time away from her, V could gain control of her emotions, steel herself to endure the inevitable heartbreak when Jewel returned to Earth.

After her allotted time, the shower turned off and a blast of hot air hit her. When the stall lifted, a beautiful woman stood before her. Jewel, in all of her naked glory.

"I guess those showers weren't meant for two."

V smiled. "No, but feel free to have one."

"I'd rather have you again."

Heat traveled straight to V's apex. All of her resolve flittered away in an instant.

Jewel quickly took control, pressing her against the wall and claimed her mouth. Work could wait. She'd take as much as she could get while Jewel remained at the space station, and maybe she'd find a way for her to stay.

Jewel lifted her leg onto the shower platform. She kissed her way down V's stomach. Kneeling in front of her, she slipped fingers into swollen tissues wet in anticipation. As Jewel pressed her tongue against her swollen nub, she gasped. How could she ever deny she wanted her guest?

Sliding two fingers into the moistness between her legs, Jewel continued to tease her clit, licking and sucking. She lost herself in ecstasy. Her muscles tightened around Jewel's fingers. So close to her release, she held the woman's head in place.

Jewel sucked harder, her fingers sinking deep into her heat. V ground against her mouth...her fingers...finally erupting in a dizzying explosion of feeling. "Fuck," she gasped, trying to catch her breath.

Firm breasts against hers, Jewel's smooth forehead pressed to hers. "You okay?"

She bit her lip and nodded. *No, I don't want you to leave. I won't last here without you.*

Hand in hand, they returned to her bed and lay wrapped in each other. Minutes, maybe an hour passed before she peeled away. She would go to work, even though she'd not been scheduled, before her resolve melted once more.

Jewel kissed her then leaned down to grab her clothes. "Can we visit Carrie and Frey today? When you were in the bathroom earlier, I got a message on my communicator saying Carrie had her baby. She's been moved to the medical bay."

"Really?" How could Jewel be so excited when their time together was running out? But getting away from her was what V needed right now.

"That's what the message said. I'd really like to see their baby, hold it in my arms."

V turned away. "Sure, I'll take you, but I have to go in to work for a few hours." She couldn't see Jewel holding a baby. The sight would only make things worse, make her want even more things she couldn't have.

She dressed for work then ordered breakfast for the two of them from the replicator.

Jewel moaned as she forked food into her mouth. "This food is really good, not bland like they said in training at all. How do they make it?"

"I don't know." She didn't want to explain the technology, trying to gain some distance. Jewel would probably have her date, spend the night elsewhere and leave the next day, never to see her again.

When they approached the tubes, she went first to demonstrate to Jewel how to use them on her own—and to resist touching her again. She led her charge, her one-time lover, to Carrie's hospital room and left without saying good-bye.

As she rode the tube to work, she let the pneumatic suction whisk her tears away.

Chapter Nine

Jewel turned to speak to V, but she had already left. She didn't understand V's cold demeanor after they'd been together again in the bathroom. She'd barely said a word, making Jewel wonder if everything they'd shared had been an act on her part. She didn't want to misread her again, but what was she supposed to think when V hadn't said goodbye? Not even a "see you later."

She focused on the little blue baby girl in Frey's arms. With only slightly longer arms and legs, she looked like a human baby, save for her blue skin and pure black eyes. Carrie slept in the bed nearby.

"She's the first blonde Ginnunian." His dark eyes shone bright with pride.

Jewel smiled. "Yes, she looks so much like her mother."

"Her name is Tabitha." Frey set the baby girl in her arms. "Sit down, and tell me how your stay's been so far."

"Well, V took me to a dance club, and we had a great time." She opened up, the baby in her arms making her feel like part of a family again. Her strange experience on the space station would be something she could never talk to anyone on Earth about. Yet somehow, she felt more comfortable there than back home. *I don't want to leave. Everything that makes me happy is here, although it's only been one night. I don't feel different. I can be me and not have to worry about being labeled as a monster.*

When two communicators beeped at the same time, Frey took Tabitha and placed her in a bassinette then reached for his comm. Jewel read the message on her device.

You must return to Earth. Now! An escort is waiting to take you to the portal.

She gasped, thinking of V. She'd never get to see her again. At a knock, she stood, and moved toward the door, fear and regret clutching her heart.

A Phantie guard stood outside. "Ms. Barnaby, I need you to come with me. Mr. Berger, will you and your family be coming?"

He looked at Carrie then Tabitha. "No, it's better for us to stay here. Be sure she gets home safely."

The Phantie nodded then escorted her out of the room. He wasn't as gentle as V had been in leading her through the tube. Thank goodness he didn't land on her when they reached their destination. She would have been crushed by his weight.

A swirling circle in a room off of the concourse waited to take her back to Earth. She had no idea why she had to leave early. The Phantie refused to tell her.

"You need to go home," he said, leading her through the large hall.

But she didn't want to leave. V's smiling face had greeted her when she'd arrived only the day before. And now she had to leave without seeing her again?

She turned around, hoping to find V behind her, coming with her. No such luck.

The Phantie shoved her closer to the portal. She spun on her heels. *I have to see her before I go.* She couldn't leave without saying good-bye, without knowing if she'd ever see her again. Surely she could find the hotel V worked at or at least ask for directions.

She reached the concourse before the Phantie caught her. Unlike the first time she'd arrived there, the grand room stood empty, red light flashing throughout.

"What's going on?"

He grabbed her around the waist, carrying her in a football hold toward the portal. "You need to go home." He set her down in front of the swirling mass and pushed her through.

Her body tightened. Pressure rammed against her head until she thought her brain would explode. The trip to the space station hadn't felt like this. *Oh, shit. Something is wrong.* Tears rolled down her face. Her heart pounded, ready to jump out of her chest. *It hurts so much.* She saw a light ahead and reached out. Then darkness consumed her.

☙

V was sitting on the toilet, wiping her nose with tissue when her communicator beeped. She didn't want to talk to anyone, to face anyone. She wanted to go home, back to Earth, and be with Jewel.

The device beeped again.

Director's office. Now!

Shit! What had she done wrong? No one received a message to report to the director's office unless they were to be reprimanded. And she'd done as she'd been asked, entertaining Jewel all night long.

But then again, she'd abandoned her at the hospital. Then there was the date.... Had the wrong person seen them at the club last night? Had someone reported what happened between them?

She swiped at her eyes and nose one last time before leaving the bathroom. *Time to face the music.* In no way did she regret what had happened between her and Jewel; she only wished they'd had more time together. *Why did I leave her?* She vowed to find Jewel after her meeting with the director, to spend every last minute with her.

The tube dropped her outside the office. Her hand shook on the scanner as she waited for the door to open.

"Ah, Flavia, I'm glad you're here." Instead of inviting her to sit, he got up from his chair to stand beside her, his tail dragging behind him. Worry lines showed all over his red face.

"What's going on?" she asked, her fear about being reprimanded evaporated.

"There's a situation on Earth. Terrorists have learned of our technology to travel through space." He raked a hand across the spines on top of his head. "The portal is going to be destroyed to prevent anyone else from coming across. At least for now."

She drew in a quick breath. "What about Jewel?" Would she be forced to stay?

"We sent her through already. The portal hadn't warmed up, but she made it through."

She exhaled. *At least she's safe.* "And why am I here?" How did this affect her? She couldn't return to Earth.

"We're giving you the chance to go home."

Her heart leaped from her chest. She'd never wanted anything more, yet she knew there would be a catch. "Under what conditions?"

The director chuckled, a bit of smoke escaping from his mouth. "You will still work for us. As you were recruited, you will recruit others, preparing for another passage between Earth and the space station." He handed her a new communicator. "The time has come for Earth to know about us. I will contact you soon. Right now you need to go. The portal will close in five minutes."

If he said anything else, she missed his words. She ran out of the office then slammed the tube button. When she landed, she set her sights on the passage to Earth, its mass quickly shrinking.

"Wait," she yelled at the Phantie standing by the controls. He held a large bar of steel, ready to destroy the system.

V took off running then dove when she reached the platform, hoping the portal didn't close before she traveled through.

Chapter Ten

Jewel opened her eyes, a soft hand brushing across her cheek.

"Hi, sweetie."

She gasped. "V?"

"Yeah, it's me."

"But...I thought...." She reached out then pulled V down against her. "I'm so glad you're here." But had she made it back to Earth or was she still on the space station? She didn't care because she had V in her arms.

☙

She let Jewel hold her for as long as she wanted, for she wanted to be there just as much.

"Where are we?" Jewel asked once she let her go.

"Back on Earth. At the lab where the portal *was*." Although the section they stayed in remained quiet, the rest of the lab raced to tear apart the equipment before the technology could be used to harm rather than help.

"Are you here for good?" Hope filled her voice. "Or do you have to go back?"

She ran a hand across Jewel's forehead, stroking away a few strands of hair. "I'm here for now. Eventually I may have to go back, but not until they rebuild the portal." Returning to the space station held no appeal anyway, unless they went together. So long as they could build something from the night they'd spent together.

The door to the room opened to admit a man in camo fatigues toting an automatic weapon. "Ladies, your ride is here. You need to move, now."

"Jewel, are you okay to walk?" She'd wanted to say more, discuss their future, but they'd run out of time.

"I...I don't know."

She scooped her off the cot and into her arms. Following their escort, she rushed through the halls then outside, Jewel clinging to her.

When they reached the limousine, V set her on the seat then climbed in beside her.

"The director will be in touch." Their escort closed the door then tapped on the trunk.

V should have been worried with all of the extra security around the lab compound, but her stomach churned as a result of the woman beside her. Their future together, unknown.

"Where are we going?" Jewel, buckled in beside her, leaned on her shoulder.

"You're going home."

"And you?"

Only one destination came to mind. Wherever Jewel went. "I assume the Space Service will find me accommodations."

Jewel sat up and took her hand. "You're welcome to stay with me. I don't have an extra bedroom or anything, but I do have room in my bed."

Smiling, V squeezed her hand. Exactly what she'd hoped for.

"That is, if you want to be seen with the town monster."

She leaned over and captured Jewel's mouth with her own for a tantalizing kiss. Never again would she let her woman think of herself as a monster. Pulling away, she stroked the side of her face. "I do want to be with you, but perhaps we could find a two bedroom place in Ottawa?"

"Two bedroom?"

"Well, for now." She smiled. "You know, one for us and the other one we'll use as an office. And in the future—"

Her communicator beeped. A message came in from the director.

I'm glad to hear you're safely back on Earth. Frey and Carrie would like you to house sit for them while they remain at the space station. Do you accept?

Yes, she replied. Much better than an apartment.

She watched Jewel reading a message on her phone, her lips spreading into a huge smile. Then she let V read the message.

Darling Jewel,

I'm very sorry your time on the space station was cut short. And yet you still managed to meet with your one-night stand.

Yes, Flavia was the woman you were sent to meet. The director and I believed you would complement each other well. And we are overjoyed you are together now.

All the best in the future,

Madame Evangeline

With a heavy chest, V vowed not to cry. Now was a time to be happy. Someone named Madame Evangeline, along with the director had made all of her dreams come true. But who was that mysterious woman? She sighed. Right now, she had other things to concentrate on. She'd returned to Earth and had a beautiful woman in her life. Her future became a little less unknown.

She wrapped an arm around Jewel, pulling her closer then kissed her. "Let's go home." And perhaps on the way, she'd remind her lover of the beauty she saw when she looked at her.

Satin Sheets in Space

Chapter One

Danyka's eyes flew open. The phone danced around on her nightstand. The numbers on her alarm clock blurred and came into focus. Seven o'clock. *Shit!* She'd meant to nap for an hour, but had slept for three. She fumbled for the device, but it stopped before she could reach it.

Eighties pop music jived from her Android again, sending it into another jig. Grabbing the phone, she pressed it against her head. "Hello?"

"Dany, where are you?" Her friend, Ellie, squealed on the other end.

Danyka yanked the phone from her ear and rubbed, before listening again.

"We're waiting outside—in the limo."

Double shit. She needed a shower and time to dress in her eighteenth-century inspired designer gown. Closing her eyes, she pinched the bridge of her nose and fell back on the bed, staring at the ceiling, trying to gain some control over her body. "Give me half an hour to get ready. Can you come back?"

Ellie sighed. "Fine, it's your dollar. See you in a bit."

No, it wasn't her dollar, but her boss's. Personal assistant to Josh Summers, film producer, she'd intended to enjoy her two weeks off—while he traveled across Europe on his honeymoon—

and her sizable bonus. She'd picked up the envelope that had held the extra cash and three tickets to the Kartha Studio's charity ball and pulled out a note.

Danyka,

Take two friends and have fun! Connie from Connie's Couture, will take care of all of your gowns, and a limo will provide transportation there and home (if you need it then). Enjoy yourself while I'm gone, because we'll be working crazy hours when Tamara and I get back.

Thanks for your dedication these last two years!

Josh

She'd fist-pumped the air before spinning in circles around her apartment when she'd read it. The ball would be A-list celebrities and industry giants from wall-to-wall. She'd phoned her friends, Ellie and Vanessa, right away, barely able to contain her excitement. But when they'd visited Connie's to find dresses, she'd been filled with a sense of dread, reminded again of her freakish size. While she'd been granted womanly curves and a considerable bust, she towered over most men. She even had a couple of inches on Josh.

He'd never seemed to care, but when it came to finding a boyfriend, or even a date, her options were limited. Any guy she'd met taller than herself seemed to prefer women half her size. Those shorter than her gawked from a distance, but their eyes bulged out of their sockets when she approached them. On occasion, a short slimeball would come on to her, wondering what it would be like to *do* a giant. There would be civilized, respectable men at the ball. At least, she hoped so. In the end though, she expected to spend the night alone.

Her friends had found their dream gowns after trying on what seemed like hundreds of dresses, but she hadn't had a single choice. There had been one she'd admired. Connie took her measurements and promised to search for a similar one in her size. Instead, on the day she went to pick it up, the woman had surprised her with a custom-made dress.

Sliding off the bed, she groaned. Her knees were already sore from the impending precipitation. Her joints were as good a gauge as any other high-tech gadget to measure the barometric pressure. Plus, she planned to wear heels the entire night, making it a double-whammy. *There had better be someplace to sit down, because it's not as if anyone is going to ask me to dance anyway.*

After a quick shower, she pinned her hair up, sprinkled glitter all over, and slipped on a black thong. Then she carefully placed her pasties. *Okay, time for the gown.*

Unzipping the polyester bag, she gasped. The magnificence of the dress still shocked her every time she saw it. She brushed her hand across the pleated red silk of the skirt. But she didn't have time to bask in its elegance. At least not until she had it on. She stepped into her red net petticoat, sliding it up to her waist, and spun in a circle. Oh, how she missed her childhood ballet classes. Even then, she'd towered over the rest of the students. Though classes hadn't made her any less clumsy, as her parents had hoped, the friends she'd made there never let her believe she was anything less than a prima ballerina. As they pirouetted in front of the mirrors, in leotards and tutus, she'd forget her size.

With her stature and blazing auburn hair, she always attracted unfavorable attention. Tonight, though, she wanted people to stare, and maybe, just maybe, her knight in shining armor would arrive to sweep her off her feet.

She wiggled the skirt on and brushed her hands down the material to smooth it out. *Almost ready.*

Deciding to forgo the detachable straps, Danyka wrapped the red silk corset around her torso, buttoning it up in the front. With a squeal of delight, she raced to the mirror.

She couldn't help but twirl like a little girl. Before this moment, nothing in her life had resembled a fairy tale, except landing the position as Josh's assistant. At the age of sixteen, she'd been orphaned when her parents died in a horrific car accident. Her aunt had agreed to take her in, rather than sending her to a group home, but the woman had spent as little time with her as possible, always busy planning some *important* event.

With her back toward the mirror, Danyka caught sight of the ink on her right shoulder. The Milky Way—a tribute to her and her dad's shared love for space and science fiction. The day she'd come home with her first tattoo, her aunt had decided she should find an apartment of her own. Lucky for her, Ellie and Vanessa, classmates from the University of Nevada, Las Vegas, had needed a roommate. They'd since graduated and found their own places, but remained close as they made their way in the *real world.*

She suspected her interests made her a perfect fit for Josh, a former sci-fi television star, now producing his own space flick. The tattoo had never bothered him, but would it be inappropriate at a charity ball? Why hadn't she thought of that earlier? She didn't have time to have her mark covered up. No, the ink would be just another way for her to stand out in the crowd.

Once she'd applied her make-up, she fished in her closet and pulled out her brand new black slingbacks—matching the lacing on the back of her dress—still in their box. They'd probably be off again in a couple of hours. She and heels never got along. When she opened the box, a small brown paper package lay on top. *Where did that come from?*

The bag felt weightless in her palm. She removed a small piece of tape, letting a handkerchief and note fall to the floor. The red silk material could have been made from the same fabric as her dress, her initials DAR embroidered in the corner with black thread. Combined with the gown, shoes, and her awaiting carriage, the silk accessory completed her transformation into a princess. All she needed was a Prince Charming.

After a quick glance at the clock, she picked up the note. She had seconds to read it before fashionably late turned into rude. Although the paper came from Josh's personalized notepad, the handwriting did not match that of her boss.

Danyka,

I hope you enjoy yourself at the Kartha Ball tonight! As we figured Ellie and Vanessa would be going with you, we have an extra special surprise for you and you alone. Although Josh and I don't discuss this with anyone, we met through a dating service called 1Night Stand. The owner, Madame Evangeline, has matched up not only us, but many of my close friends. We have arranged for you to go on one of these dates tonight. We hope we have not overstepped our bounds, but we consider you part of our family and want to see you happy.

Your date, whoever he may be, will meet you at the ball.

Have a wonderful time, and enjoy the rest of your holidays!

Tamara

They had arranged a date for her? She restrained the urge to jump up and down and whoop in delight, blowing out a breath and remaining calm. Another part of her cringed. Was she so desperate she had to rely on a matchmaking service to find a man? A one-night stand at that?

Her gaze shifted to her nightstand, the drawer inside filled with vibrators, rubber dildos, and more. Oh yeah, that screamed desperation. *All right, Eve, bring on a real man.*

She set the note down on the bed. Grabbing her clutch on the way out the door, she couldn't help but smile. She might not be off to meet the man she would marry, but she hoped to end the night completely satisfied.

☙

Galan drummed his fingers against the counter. He hadn't expected to have such a hard time finding eighteenth century dress, specifically a knee-length justacorps-style coat and breeches. It wasn't that he couldn't find any, but none of the costume shops he'd visited had anything in his size. His thighs prevented him from wearing most pants, and the width of his back caused coat after coat to rip in the seams. *Did they grow them that small here?*

At last, he'd found the perfect costume for the ball at a quaint boutique named Connie's Couture. The elegant black outfit, with red silk shirt and stockings, seemed to have been tailored for him, although he'd never been to this area during his travels.

Connie remained in the back, completing some last minute adjustments to his clothing, while he ran through his mental list of everything he needed to purchase before he met his date. *Flowers, breath mints...what else?*

A hotel room waited for them at the Castillo Hotel, where the ball would take place, but he planned to take his date elsewhere, if she agreed. Traveling as much as he did, he grew lonely and wanted someone to share the wondrous places he often visited. His brother as his companion wasn't enough. No, he wanted a woman to settle down with rather than finding a new source of temporary satisfaction at every port.

During his last stopover, he'd avoided all his and Volan's usual haunts, instead spending his evenings on the beaches of Somnium, contemplating his life. And his next voyage. A friend of a friend had recommended the 1Night Stand dating service he'd heard about on Earth. Still, he'd had reservations. He wasn't like any of the men he'd met around the Terran city of Las Vegas. But he'd filled out the forms, and learned yesterday about his date.

His life had been a scramble since, with no time to inform his brother of his plans. What would Volan think of the arrangement? He'd been quite happy with a variety of women, and never hinted at the need to settle down. Would his brother be respectful of his change in lifestyle? Didn't matter. He'd already made his decision, so long as his date went well. He needed something different. Maybe his conversion would influence Volan to commit to one woman.

"All set, Mr. Galan." Connie rushed from the back room, a black polyester bag across her arm. "I hope you have a wonderful time at the ball tonight and charm the lucky woman you're going to meet."

He smiled, setting additional currency on the counter to compensate the woman for her extra time and attention. Clasping her by the shoulders, he air-kissed her cheeks in the same way she'd greeted him when he arrived. "Thank you, Ms. Connie. I appreciate all your time. Now, I must get going, as I am already very late."

She handed him the bag. "Why don't you change here? The Castillo is a block away, and this way I can see my hard work."

He hoped his date would be as sweet as the woman before him. "That would be great. Thank you, again."

She ushered him toward a closet-sized room, closing the curtain behind him. She'd already demonstrated how to dress in the period costume, so he donned the outfit in minimal time. The breeches cupped him with precision, as he decided to forgo traditional undergarments. He stared at his reflection. Perhaps he could fit in at the ball, dressed as an eighteenth century Terran, long enough to woo the woman who waited for him.

Exiting the changing room, Galan stood in the middle of the store, waiting for Connie's approval. "Well?"

"If I didn't have a charming man of my own, I'd hope I was your date for the ball." She handed him a small plastic container, holding a delicate red rose.

"What's this?" He'd expected to buy a bouquet of flowers rather than just one. What would he do with one tiny flower?

"It's for her wrist. I know it's not fitting to the time period, but I'm sure she'll love it."

He took the container from her, kissing her on the cheek this time. "I appreciate all you've done for me. I'm glad to have met you."

She nodded. "Now go, before she thinks you've stood her up."

Rushing out the door, he set his sights on the Castillo Hotel, lights shining brighter than any other on the strip. Long, black cars still arrived with men and woman dressed for the ball. *Good. I'm not late.*

He hurried into the hotel and to the ball room, flashing his invitation at the door. He'd made sure to grab it before leaving Connie's Couture but left his regular clothing there. He wouldn't need any of the local fashions anyway, for he planned on leaving in the morning. He only hoped his date would come along for the trip.

Searching the room, worry gnawed at his gut. None of the women inside suited his preferences. Had Madame Evangeline made a mistake? He ducked his head under the ivy-laced trellis to step in farther. He'd been told his date would come up past his stomach. There had to be a woman on Earth fitting that description, and he trusted she waited for him in the room.

Chapter Two

Danyka plopped onto the cushioned banquet chair. She'd been on her feet for two hours, mingling with industry professionals. And waiting for her date. At this point, she'd given up on him. He'd either stood her up or spied her from across the room and scurried away. Josh and Tamara had good intentions, but they'd left her disappointed.

She removed her shoes, sighing as her feet returned to their normal size. Blisters stung below her ankles and on her little toes. *How can anyone wear these all day?*

After sitting down for a few minutes, she contemplated leaving. She had nothing to look forward to for the rest of the night, only a constant reminder of her loneliness. Leaning back, she caught a glimpse of a multitude of stars through the skylights in the arched ceiling. Focusing on the celestial objects allowed her to forget where she was for a moment, at least until someone shoved her into the table as he passed behind her.

"Watch where you're going." *Sheesh.* He'd had plenty of room to move between the tables, but no, he had to bump into her.

The man stumbled to glare back at her. "If you took up less space, I wouldn't have tripped over you. You're lucky I don't sue."

Sighing, she rolled her eyes. There had to be someplace on Earth, or in the universe, where women over five-foot-six weren't seen as Amazons. She turned to the dance floor and watched Vanessa and Ellie, in their corsets and long, heavy skirts, gyrating against their own princes. Charming, maybe, but the up-and-coming movie stars acted more like overgrown teenagers on set, playing practical jokes and sharing more of their personal lives than she cared to know. But when her friends had begged to meet them, she'd caved to their wishes.

The boys enjoyed the attention and had already asked Vanessa and Ellie to escort them to the after party. Which meant they'd become another tick on their scorecards, but she couldn't tell them any different. They enjoyed the buzz, the attention.

Like most nights she went out with the girls, Danyka hadn't been asked to dance. She would have been happy even if someone besides her date had asked. Instead, she sat watching, wishing she were anyone else. Tonight, she hadn't even needed to act as their DD, designated divider. When her friends needed help getting away from guys who thought they were going to get laid, but hadn't a hope in hell, she would run interference. No, tonight she had lost all hope.

Her vibrator called to her, the sole object that continued to bring her pleasure. Why couldn't she be asked to dance? Once was all she asked for. Instead men went for her shorter companions with big boobs flowing out of their corsets, girls who looked like dainty, damsels-in-distress tonight. She'd never needed anyone to rescue her, but just once, she'd like someone to offer.

Ellie turned to wave at her as the group of four made their way to the exit. She wouldn't see them again tonight.

That's it, I'm leaving. She didn't need to stick around and be reminded of another night she'd been stood up by a blind date and passed over by every other available male.

After slipping her shoes on and grabbing her clutch, she headed for the door.

"Leaving so soon?"

She shivered at the sound of the deep, sexy voice. Spinning around, she gazed up at an enormous, captivating man. Very rarely did she meet a guy so much taller than herself. His black velvet justacorps fit tight across his broad shoulders, but not too snug. And the silk shirt lining his wide chest matched the color of her dress. Almost as if they were made for each other. *I can only hope.*

Flowing down his back, his long, thick, dark mane appeared to have feathers throughout. In the dim lighting, his hair, and even his skin had a faint blue glow. She couldn't help but be enthralled by his presence; was sure she stood in front of him with her mouth hanging open.

"I...I'm going home."

"When the night is still so young?" He brushed his hand down her bare arm. "What could be more fun at home? Perhaps you might even enjoy some company?"

How she'd love to spend the night in this man's company, the toys in her nightstand long forgotten. But this had to be some kind of joke. She looked around for cameras, anxious faces. No one as hot as this man could want to spend a night with *her*. "It's been a long day. I was stood up by my date, and my friends no longer need me to stick around."

Great! She'd just told the guy she was alone. *Might as well have put a target on my back.*

He rested his hand on her hip, sending intense sexual energy zinging straight to her core. "You mean you wouldn't want to enjoy an evening in my company? Because I'm your date."

He brought her hand up to kiss her knuckles, his lips soft against her skin.

What would they feel like elsewhere?

He slid a red rose corsage onto her wrist, marking her as his. She didn't care to object. "I'm sorry I made you think I wasn't coming. I...I had a hard time finding a costume that fit. So, will you consider spending the rest of the night with me?"

Consider? *God, yes!* She'd considered it the moment she'd heard his voice, but didn't believe he would want to spend any time with her. And she could relate to the search to find proper-sized clothing. Madame Evangeline *had* found her perfect match. But could she go through with the date? *Yes! Time to take a chance.*

"What do you have in mind?"

Pulling her against his hard physique, he grinned. "Perhaps some dancing? After that, we'll see where things go."

She tingled in anticipation. A year had passed since she'd last had sex with a guy, and he'd only been in it for himself, leaving her bed after coming all over her chest. But this man had the potential to give her so much more, his touch making her body hum in silent longing. Should she get her hopes up? Could she have found her ideal man, even for one night?

"I...sure, I guess." Her cheeks warmed as he released her. Then he bowed and held out his hand for hers.

Next to him, she felt dainty, delicate. Where had he been all her life?

She frowned. He hadn't told her his name. The wheels turned in her mind. Was that his way of preventing anything past tonight? So she couldn't look him up? She'd enjoy her time with him anyway.

He escorted her toward the dance floor, cradling her arm as she balanced on her heels. She never wore shoes that made her appear taller. Why had she decided to wear the slingbacks? She had plenty of flat, wide footwear at home. But her date's simple touch made her forget the pain in her knees and feet, and that she was taller than every woman in the room. She could concentrate on him and the possibilities of what he might do to her later in the evening.

With typical eighteenth century formal minuets playing, Mr. Tall, Dark, and Handsome held her at a respectable distance, sweeping her across the room, making her feel like royalty. Attendees cleared a path as her date twirled her across the floor, and those around the tables stared. But she didn't care. She kept her focus on the man holding her, returning his radiant smile. She'd watched enough of the dancing to know she had the best partner in the room. He moved with grace and finesse, a result of either ballroom lessons or a mother who taught her son how to treat a lady. Either way, he was hers for the night. One magical night.

"And now to wrap up the ball, we're going to play more modern music," the disc jockey announced. "Enjoy your evening, ladies and gentlemen."

Danyka recognized the song in an instant, one she'd often listened to, talking of angels and aliens. *Hardly modern, but at least from the last century.*

Her partner for the evening pulled her close as the music slowed. "Thank the gods they changed the music. I need to be closer to you."

Gods? A different religion, perhaps? She didn't care. Desire coursed through her from head to toe. He could touch and taste every inch, without any objection from her.

He leaned down, his warm breath grazing her neck. Her nipples perked, pressed against his hard body.

"I noticed the galaxy on your shoulder."

She sighed with disappointment, having expected him to kiss her. "Yes, I have a tattoo."

Would a little ink stand in their way? She tried to pull away, to brace for his dismissal, but his hold on her never faltered.

"I like it. Why did you choose the Milky Way?"

Releasing the breath she'd been holding, Danyka smiled with relief. Her cheeks ached from the joy this man brought her. "It's a tribute to my father. We'd often lie on the back lawn and watch the stars. He taught me about the constellations in our galaxy, and many other celestial bodies throughout the universe."

A wave of sadness washed over her. She missed those moments, and her father.

Her date brushed his thumb along her cheek, bringing her attention back to him. "And what did he teach you about the possibility of other life—out in space?"

Did she really want to ruin this evening with talk of her belief in aliens? *No.*

He raised his eyebrows, waiting for an answer.

Oh hell. "He told me not to assume Earth is the only planet in the universe capable of sustaining life."

"So you believe?"

"In a matter of speaking, yes." There, she'd said it. *Now watch him run.* "But I can't say I've ever met anyone from another world."

His placed gentle kisses across her neck, lighting a fire deep in her core. "I believe, too."

Even though no distance existed between their bodies, his kiss caught her by surprise. Any self-doubt she held onto melted away, giving room to the need to be with this man. His lips, as soft as when they'd pressed against her knuckles, stole her breath away.

He pulled back, leaving her body tingling. "Perhaps we could go someplace we could have some privacy?"

The idea both scared and thrilled her. She had never been one to do anything without meticulous planning, another reason she'd never had much fun in her life. But the evening had been one big whirlwind up until now. "Let's go."

Her date held her hand with a firm grip, but not hard enough to hurt.

In a wave of panic, she stopped. She didn't even know his name. *And I'm willing to go off alone with him? What am I thinking?*

She wanted to get laid, plain and simple. Opportunities like this were too rare to pass up. And they had been set up, a presumed ideal match.

"Are you coming?" He tugged on her hand, his sexy smile washing away her doubts.

She rushed through the halls beside him, anxious to experience everything he could give her. He ducked into the kitchen, giving her pause. "Are you sure we should be in here?"

"Get out of here this instant," a woman yelled, shaking her spoon at them.

Her date laughed, taking her further into the room, toward another door. They burst through the exit, out into the cool night air. Into an alley.

She'd expected a hotel room, a car, at least, not some lane behind the hotel among garbage bins filled with rotting food.

But she had no time to object. He pinned her up against the brick wall with his body, holding her hands above her head.

He kissed her, no, devoured her. He tasted her with his lips, his tongue plunging inside her mouth, beginning an erotic dance.

She became lost in the moment, unable to form a clear or coherent thought.

Even through layers of clothing, his hard cock pressed against her stomach. She wanted him now, didn't care where they were.

As if reading her mind, he reached down, gathering her skirt. Goosebumps formed on her exposed legs from the cool breeze. But the heated desire racing through her body from his ravishing mouth burned them away with haste. She'd never been kissed so passionately.

With one hand holding her skirt tight, he slid his other between her legs, trailing his hand along the cloth of her thong. She shivered, awaiting penetration of any kind. She creamed against the small piece of fabric as he rubbed her swollen mound.

"Oh, that's what I like." He reached down to catch the juices running down her leg then grabbed a handful of material and ripped. "But these were getting in the way."

Tossing her underwear away, he explored her slick folds. She whimpered as he brushed his finger along her clit. She wanted more, all of him. When he slid his digit inside, she moaned, her core tightening around him. *Finally.*

He kissed along her neck, nipping her skin, intensifying her pleasure. Two more fingers slipped into her. Weak-kneed, she rode up and down his digits, intense pressure welling deep within. She sucked in short, sharp breaths. Too much time had passed since she'd had anything but toys and her own appendages touching her most intimate spots.

In a blinding explosion, she released. "God, yes!"

She rode the exhilarating wave as he continued to pump her. Her muscles relaxed, but she still yearned for him. Their night had just begun.

"Why don't we go somewhere else and continue this? We can get a room if you want." She didn't care where as long as they were off the street and had a little more privacy. The possibility of someone catching them excited her, but she didn't want the rest of their time together interrupted.

"I have the perfect place, *if* you're willing to trust me."

How could she? She'd just met him, didn't even know his name. Yet she refused to say no, couldn't have him walk away and leave her alone and needy. She'd go wherever he wanted to take her, whether to a bondage dungeon or a closet. So long as he took her, over and over. Because, for once, she'd found a guy who pleasured her without her asking. She planned to return the favor as soon as they left the alley.

With one hand gripping her ass, he skimmed a finger back across her slick folds. "Well, do you?"

Only aware of her growing need, she nodded.

He returned to her slippery heat, plunging in and out. "First, tell me your name."

"Danyka." Her name rolled out as she moaned with his movements.

"Okay, Danyka, hold onto me."

How could she not? He'd transformed her knees, her entire body, to jelly with his touch. She already gripped his sleeves, afraid if she let go she'd fall, slide down the wall.

Pulling some kind of remote from his pocket, he pressed the single white button on its surface. He slipped the device back into his pouch then leaned forward to reclaim her mouth.

She had her eyes closed, her lips pressed against his, when the sensation started. First, a tingling in her hands and feet, as he swept his digits deep inside her. The buzz spread up her arms and legs until it engulfed her entire body. She no longer sensed the ground below her.

The man continued to drive his fingers into her core with vigor, ridding her of the urge to pull away and find out what was happening to her. She landed with a thud, feeling returning to her limbs. Nothing stopped the man who held her, though. He continued to ravage her mouth, her jaw, her neck, keeping her pressed against the wall.

But something felt different. Gone was the hard brick pressing through her corset and against her skin. She reached behind to brush her hand along the surface. Soft. Almost like cushioned satin.

With a whimper, she pushed the strange man away. Where was she? What had she been thinking? *This is the stupidest, most insane thing I've ever done.*

The Prince Charming she'd had the fortune of being set up with peered down at her, his gaze intense and filled with lust. "My name is Galan, and we're in my spaceship."

At least she now knew his name, but wait.... Spaceship? She stared at the man, disillusioned. She could think of no other explanation for how they had traveled to a new location with the press of a button. Oh God, she'd been abducted by an alien. How would she get out of this situation? The first time she'd done something spur-of-the-moment, and she'd ended up being finger-fucked by an extraterrestrial.

Or was this some kind of elaborate stunt Josh had pulled off? But why? He was on his honeymoon, unable to enjoy his handiwork. Her body grew numb; a loud ringing pierced her eardrums. She could no longer think with the clouds invading her mind. Then she blacked out.

Chapter Three

If he hadn't tasted her on his lips, felt the bulge of his groin, Galan would have thought this all a dream. But no, the striking young Terran woman who'd captured his gaze from across the hall was his date for the evening, his one-night stand. Would she agree to something more, especially now she knew who and what he was? By her reaction, he didn't expect so. She'd passed out, gone limp in his arms. He laid her on his bed, contemplating whether to return her to the planet. But if he did, she'd leave his life forever. The thought made his heart ache.

From the moment he'd laid eyes on her, he understood why they'd been matched. She'd towered over almost everyone in the room. But it had been the tendrils of red hair spiraling past her cheeks, and the way she'd gazed up into the sky with complete wonder that had captivated him. He couldn't let her go. Not until she refused him outright. Until then, he'd do everything he could to ensure she stayed.

"Galan, what took you so long? Did you change your mind and sample the many fine women of this planet?"

Glaring at his twin brother, Volan, he charged over to him. "Get out of here. I don't need you to ruin this for me."

How would Danyka react if she saw two aliens?

Volan rested his hands on his shoulders, peering past him.

"Ruin what? Did you really bring one back?" He shoved Galan aside. "You did, you sly fiend. Of all the planets to find a woman, you had to pick one where they don't know about us yet?"

Galan lunged to intercept his brother before he could get a closer look. "I said, get out of here. You'll just make things worse when she wakes up."

With a laugh, Volan raised his arms and backed away. "Did you have to knock her out to get her up here?"

Anger boiled deep inside. How could he accuse him of such a thing? "No, she passed out when I told her we were on my spaceship."

"Brother, you've brought alien abduction to a whole new level." He sniffed the air. "She's highly aroused and I can't deny her beauty. Perhaps I could help convince her to stay?"

He considered the offer. After all, they had shared plenty of women during their travels. But was Volan ready to settle down? And would Danyka consider sex with two space travelers? He had to get her back to consciousness first and convince her he wouldn't bring her harm.

Danyka moaned and turned onto her side.

A swell of panic rose inside Galan. He had to plead with her to stay and accompany him around the universe. "No, not yet. I need to be alone with her right now."

"If she stays, she's going to find out about me."

"I know, but I have to do this myself."

His brother nodded and left the room.

Galan removed his waistcoat and slid onto the bed beside her. His cock twitched as he drew in her scent. Delicious, like the berry-filled pies he'd caught a whiff of on her planet. He could also smell her intoxicating scent of arousal. Why on Earth would she have to use a dating service to find someone to love?

As he leaned closer to kiss her cheek, her eyes flew open, wide with fear.

Alien? She'd been abducted by an alien? Sure, she'd fantasized about having sex with an extraterrestrial during many sessions with her dildo but hadn't expected her dreams to become reality. And she swore she'd heard two males talking rather than one as she woke. A hallucination? Her cheek warmed as a hand pressed against it. She opened her eyes.

Nope, all real from the hotter-than-hell alien lying beside her to the cherry red silk-lined room. On the apparent spaceship. Although darker than her dress, their surroundings matched her most comfortable pair of pajamas back home. Had he rummaged through her belongings as she lay unconscious?

Her stomach clenched. What did he want with her? Were they on a medical probing ship? She could handle his fingers, his ravaging tongue, and the sizable cock he'd pressed against her, but she didn't want to be part of some alien experiment. "T...take me back to Earth."

He straddled her, resting on his hands and knees. Sexual energy radiated off him, weakening her resolve. He ran his tongue along her lips, reigniting her need. She lost the will to fight, if she had any at all, and accepted the slow, tender kiss he offered.

Her pussy ached to be filled. Maybe she could spend some more time on this spaceship—at least long enough to experience the rest of him.

She gasped as he pulled away.

"Don't you want to see where this goes? I have so much to offer you, and I promise you won't regret staying."

Breaking their connection seemed to have cleared her head, at least a bit. She inched out from underneath him, sitting up and gaining some distance. "I...I do. It's just...alien? Really?"

His large brown eyes turned glassy. "I am, and if you'd like to return, I understand. I don't want you to think you're trapped here. I could never do that to you."

She breathed in deep. He'd stirred her guilt. She understood the pain of rejection. How could she do that to another, even if he wasn't from Earth?

"I...I want to know more...about you, about where you come from." Then, maybe, the entire situation wouldn't seem so bizarre.

His lips twisted into a smile. "I'm Perrotian, from the galaxy of the same name, fifteen light years away. There are a few life-sustaining planets there, but I've never been one to settle down, that is, until now."

Her heart fluttered. "You're going to stay on Earth?"

"No." Taking her hand, he stroked the back with his thumb. "I want someone to share the beauty of the universe with."

Soaring through the stars had always been a dream, but the hefty cost of a seat aboard any commercial space flight kept her on the ground. Even though she had no relatives she cared about on Earth, she did have friends she considered her family. Could she leave them all behind? "I—"

He reached up, placing a finger on her lips. "Shh, don't decide now. Let's spend the night together, and you can make a decision in the morning."

Before she had a chance to respond, the wall—more like a curtain—parted as another male, wearing a thin white pair of lounge pants, sauntered toward her. With the same dark mane, blue-tinged skin, and wide build, he could be a copy of the extraterrestrial that lay on the bed with her. Two alien hunks?

Part of her wanted to scream, run, get away from these men—aliens—before they tried to hurt her, or worse. But the idea of the exotic creatures excited her beyond belief.

Galan slid off the bed and stood in front of the other man. "I told you to give me some time alone with her."

"And I did." Her date's carbon copy peeked over Galan's shoulder. "Now I'm here to help you convince her to stay."

She shivered. If he was as passionate as her date, she would have one hell of a one-night stand.

Galan pushed the other man behind the curtain until they both disappeared. During their absence, she glanced around the room, searching for some sign that she truly was on a spaceship, but found nothing. Everything was warm and soft, not cold steel as she'd expected in a flying saucer.

Her date returned minutes later. He ran a hand over the top of his head and down his long strands. "My brother, he'd like to join us, to bring you added pleasure."

She raised an eyebrow as her heart hammered in her chest. How could she say no? Two times the pleasure, double the fun.

"But only if you're willing. I promise he won't hurt you." The corner of his mouth twitched. "What do you say?"

She chewed her bottom lip. If she agreed, would Galan be offended? "I'd like that if it's what you want, too."

He parted the curtain. "C'mon in, Volan."

Returning to her side, Galan ran his hand along her exposed thigh.

The new male circled the bed, examining her with his stare. "Brother, she's perfect." He brushed his fingers over her back, across her tattoo. "And marked for us, too. You chose well."

"I didn't choose, Volan. An Earth woman, albeit one with supernatural powers, set us up together. I couldn't have asked for a better match."

Her cheeks warmed with their unfamiliar compliments. She could listen to them forever.

Volan joined them on the bed. "It turns out I'm looking to settle down, like my brother. What do you say to two men bringing you pleasure, tonight? We'll make it a night you'll never forget."

She turned to Galan. Did he consent to this? Was a ménage normal for them? She'd never been with two men at the same time. And brothers at that. Her body shook with desire, imagining the fantasies the two could fulfill.

With Galan's nod, moisture flooded her thighs. She wanted them both. Even if for one night.

Chapter Four

At their request, Danyka stood beside the bed, and waited for one of the brothers to move. They stared for what seemed like hours, when in reality, seconds had passed. Finally, Volan slid off the bed and approached her from behind. She dared not move for fear she'd wake up and learn this had all been a dream. As his warm breath tickled her skin, he reached around and slid his hands inside her corset. He cupped her breasts, lifting them out of the restricting material. Kissing her neck, he worked magic across her bare flesh with his hands.

Galan drew closer, peeling off her pasties before he leaned down and sucked on her nipple. She gasped, overwhelmed by her longing, the heat invading her body.

Enhancing each sensation, Volan rubbed her other pebbled peak between his fingers. "Do you want to leave us?"

She whimpered. "No, but please don't hurt me." Her only fear of being with these aliens and two men at the same time.

Galan gazed up at her, unhooking her corset. "We could never bring you any harm. You're our *sodalis*, should you decide to stay."

His brother unzipped her skirt, letting it pool at her feet. "No, we'll never hurt you, our *sodalis*."

She didn't care what *sodalis* meant, for these two worshiped her body, their hands and mouths exploring every inch. A nip here, a squeeze there, sent her closer to release. By the time they'd laid her on the bed, they'd stripped her of all her clothing. Volan stretched his naked body beside her, his large cock jutting into her hip, and stroked her breasts. At the edge of the bed, Galan finished removing his garments. He crawled behind her, pressing his body, his ample erection against her bare ass.

How could she have gotten so lucky? Her time with these men had already lasted longer than any sexual experience she'd ever had.

Galan rolled her onto her back, claiming her mouth, his untied hair acting like a curtain to keep her focused on the moment, while his brother suckled the peaks of her breasts. No man had ever paid so much attention to her body. If a boyfriend lasted her minimum six weeks, they'd dump her after the first quick fuck. To have not one, but two men ravaging her body felt divine.

Volan kissed her stomach, nipping and licking, all the way down to her aching mound. She'd heard from her friends oral sex could be exhilarating, but none of her previous partners had ever taken the time to show her just how much. She needed more. Sliding to the end of the bed, Volan held her legs open. With the first lap of his tongue across her needy spot, she moaned into Galan's mouth.

"You like that, do you?" Galan asked.

She nodded, thrusting her hips into the air. Volan continued to savor her, pushing down on her legs.

Galan brushed his hand across her face. "Well then let's take this a step further."

Her stomach clenched as she drew in a quick breath. What did he want?

He straddled her chest, stroking his hefty cock in front of her, smearing pre-cum over the head. "Will you take me?"

She exhaled. She'd had plenty of experience in *giving* oral sex. Guys would wait for her as long as they got something in return. But she'd never sucked a cock as large or as thick. As she lifted her head to take him, he placed a soft cushion under her neck for support. He leaned forward and fucked her mouth. Keeping his movements long and slow, he never made her gag, somehow able to sense how much she could handle. And that amount grew with every thrust. Giving head to him did not feel like a chore.

With her rush of heat, Volan inserted his digits into her pussy. His fingers and magical tongue worked her closer to release. She moaned around Galan's cock, taking him farther down her throat. How could anything feel so amazing? Stroke after stroke, they plunged into her. Pressure built throughout her body, until she burst with orgasm like a Fourth of July display. Galan pulled away and sucked on her nipple, intensifying the sensations even more.

She gasped, trying to catch her breath. Never before had anyone satisfied her so much. She could stay there forever.

Galan lay on his back beside her, his mane pooled across the satin sheets. Grabbing her hips, he rolled her onto his broad, chiseled body. "I hope you can handle more of us, as we're far from finished." He reached behind her, sliding his hand down her ass and across her slick mound. "I want to feel your Terran pussy around my cock."

She shuddered, wanting him, no, needing him to fill her. Sex, when she chose to engage in it, had always felt like an obligation to any boyfriend. Not now. Not with these two men—aliens. She was living her fantasy. Although she'd never imagined the spaceship, the foreign setting added to the excitement.

Galan lifted her over his engorged flesh. Her muscles tightened as he slid into her, his cock filling her. She gasped, releasing her breath slowly. If she'd known sex with an extraterrestrial could be like this, she would have searched for one to abduct her long ago. But then, she never would have met these two. She rocked her hips, gripping his tight biceps as she rode him. Volan stood above his brother, stroking himself. She wanted to taste him, too. Leaning forward, she licked the head of his penis.

He grunted. "Suck me, Danyka. Suck me while you fuck my brother."

Letting go of Galan, she grabbed the firm flesh of Volan's ass, gripping him as she swallowed his cock. Galan pounded into her, satiating her with unbelievable bliss. Nothing on Earth had ever felt this good.

Withdrawing from her mouth, Volan bent down and kissed her with such intensity, her mind spun on a tilted axis. He pulled away, leaving her reeling for more.

She reached out to him. "I need you."

Shaking his head, he stepped off the bed. "You'll always have me if you want me. But I'm so close to release, and in your mouth is not where I want to be."

Galan reached for her, pulling her down onto his chest. He claimed her mouth with the same hunger as his brother. Volan trailed kisses down her back, pressing a finger—moist from some magical lube—against her forbidden hole.

She drew in a quick breath.

"Shh, just relax." He pushed in further, sending a sensation like no other throughout her body.

She clenched around Galan's shaft, enticing him to move faster. God, she'd never thought anything like this was possible. Two alien men found her desirable and stimulated her in every orifice. How could anything be so wrong and feel so good?

Volan slid his finger out, but Galan kept her mind on him, his kisses and each thrust of his hardness a drugging experience. She couldn't get enough.

A cold liquid slid down the crack of her ass. Volan rubbed it in and around her hole. Shit. She'd never been fucked in the ass by one guy. Having two guys inside her with larger than normal cocks would tear her apart.

She pulled away from Galan, whimpering. "I don't think I can do this."

He held her head in his hands. "We won't hurt you. Just give it a try. If you don't like it, we'll stop. My brother will go slow."

Volan massaged her butt cheeks. "What do you say, Danyka? Are you willing to try something new?"

Everything about the experience was new. Why not keep going? They hadn't hurt her thus far. "Go ahead, fuck me in the ass."

Finding liberation in her words, she leaned down and controlled the erotic kiss shared with Galan. With continuous, measured movements, she rode him, waiting for his twin to enter her illicit hole.

He pushed in, unhurried, then stopped, a firm grip on her ass. "You okay, my *sodalis*?"

Pain pierced through her, but was short-lived with the overwhelming pleasure overriding it. She moaned and pushed back, trying to take more of both men into her. They comprehended the motion and pumped into her with long, gradual strokes. Her cries of delight filled the air.

She couldn't take much more. A sudden intense pressure built inside her. She screamed in a blinding, pulsing moment of release. The brothers' movements sped up, until they groaned, exploding into her, enhancing her continuous orgasm. Slipping their cocks from her, they lay on the bed, cradling her between them. She'd been double-fucked and never felt so satisfied. She couldn't wait to experience the sensations again, but she was too spent to do anything. Closing her eyes, she drifted into slumber.

"Not so fast, Danyka." Galan brushed the sweat-soaked hair from her face.

"Yes, *sodalis*, we need to wash you now." Volan slid off the bed then scooped her into his arms. He carried her past the satin curtains to another room full of white porcelain. The entire place appeared more like a palace than the cold, sterile vehicle she'd thought a spaceship to be. In the center of the room sat a tub the size of a small pool. One of the men must have drawn it before they joined her on the bed, forever ago. She tensed, anticipating chilled water when Volan placed her into the tub. Instead, jasmine-scented warmth surrounded her. So peaceful and relaxing. Such an unexpected night. However, the brothers weren't finished. They joined her in the tub, washing her with cloths as soft as rose petals, reaching her most intimate spots. A yearning to have them both again overwhelmed her, and without her asking, they fulfilled her desires once more.

She sat against Volan as he massaged her breasts. Galan lifted her legs onto his shoulders, sucking her swollen clit. Her heart hammered in her chest. No one would ever compare to these two.

"We will love you forever, if you let us," Volan whispered. He brushed kisses along her neck, intensifying the pleasure his brother continued to build on.

She couldn't think of forever, only the here and now, and the blinding rapture of orgasm. It tore through her body as the aliens struggled to hold her between them. And when she'd relaxed, Galan continued his sexual torture with his tongue.

She shuddered. "Stop, please."

He pulled away. He set her legs down onto the textured surface of the tub and chuckled. "Not for long, my *sodalis*."

With gentle hands, the brothers spun her around until she faced Volan. "Are you up for both of us, again?"

Instead of answering him, she eased onto his cock. He released a satisfying moan as his eyes rolled back in his head. "Bless the gods we found you." He pulled her against him, claiming her mouth.

Alien or not, she couldn't get enough.

He stood, holding her against him, and she wrapped her legs around his waist. But she slid off, both their bodies slick with water. Galan caught her, grabbing her ass to prevent her landing in the tub. He helped her back onto his brother's shaft before he joined in fucking her from behind. They united in lifting her up and down their huge cocks. Over and over, her pussy and asshole clenched around them, sending her spiraling into another orgasm. Her release stole her lovers' control, and they spilled their seed deep into her.

Sinking into the still warm water, the brothers washed her all over again. A ritual she could get used to.

Spent and sated, her limbs had turned into mush. Without a word, they helped her from the bath, somehow knowing she couldn't do it on her own. They dried her off, patting every inch of her body with soft strokes. Galan swept her off her feet and into his arms, carrying her to the bed. He laid her down and crawled in beside her, draping his arm over her belly. Volan joined her on the other side, entwining his fingers with hers. She fell asleep tucked between the two males who had given her the most exhilarating experience of her entire life.

Chapter Five

Galan raised his head off the pillow. His night with Danyka had been everything he'd hoped for and more. She'd welcomed his brother to participate, important if they traveled across space together. He'd expected Volan to settle down once he'd found the right woman. And lucky for them, she had come into their lives last night.

But now, he had to complete a heart-wrenching task. He had to return Danyka to Earth, let her make the decision to return to them. They could never hold her against her will. And regret would leave her miserable. If she wanted to return to them, she would need to do it of her own free will. He hoped they'd made enough of an impression that she'd choose to soar across the universe with them.

He slid off the bed, pulled on a pair of pants, and gathered her clothing, each piece a reminder of their magical night together. He sighed; in a few minutes she'd be gone. He hoped not forever.

Volan stirred. "What are you doing?"

He placed a finger to his lips. "I'm taking her home."

"No." The sorrow across his brother's face matched every ounce of the pain piercing his heart.

"I have to, and you know it."

He scooped her up in his arms, careful not to wake her, for

saying good-bye would be that much harder.

"Will she return to us?"

He removed the transporter remote from his pocket, fingering the apparatus he'd use to bring her back if she decided to rejoin them. "I hope so." He'd already decided to postpone their departure, not wanting to leave without Danyka. Although he wouldn't wait forever.

His brother nodded. "Thank you for sharing her with me."

"Please return to your own room. When I get back, I want to be alone." He initialized the transporter system—set for the address he'd found on a card in her small bag—before he had the chance to grow selfish. Staring at the bed he'd shared with the beautiful woman in his arms, he dematerialized.

ℭ

Danyka woke in her bed, the scent of jasmine wafting through her open window. She'd had the most amazing dream, two guys fulfilling her every desire in a room lined with satin. But she couldn't remember getting home from the eighteenth century ball she'd attended with Vanessa and Ellie. They'd both left with the actors she'd introduced them to. She'd turned to leave and then....

No. The guy, Galan, he couldn't have been real. She'd concocted the fantasy to save herself from the disappointment of her date failing to show. And yet, the most erotic vision she'd ever had and so realistic with two men taking her to new heights. Her pussy still clenched at the memories. Perhaps she'd fallen at the ball, wound up with a concussion. But, how had she gotten home to bed? She had no clue.

Slipping from underneath the covers, she slid her feet into fuzzy slippers and grabbed her robe from the foot of the bed. A rose atop a piece of paper on the nightstand caught her attention. *Where did that come from?*

She picked up the note and read the distinctive handwriting.

Danyka,

Now you have met someone from another planet.

Last night was just a sample of the life we would like to have with you.

As our sodalis, *our mate, your every wish, every desire, would be ours to fulfill.*

Should you long to return to us, call our names when the night is nigh and the stars shine bright in the sky. Then we will come for you and spend a lifetime worshipping you.

Otherwise, you will soon forget about us, and we shall travel through space mourning the loss of the one we chose.

The choice is now yours.

Galan and Volan

She gasped. *It was real?*

The one night she'd decided to take a chance, to do something spontaneous, arranged by her boss and his wife, had left her more fulfilled than her entire life of meticulous planning. But could she leave her job and her friends behind? They'd been there when no one else had. But she could not deny the emptiness she felt when she returned to her apartment at night. She deserved to be happy, too. *Right?*

Her phone chimed, indicating an incoming text message. She delved into her the clutch she'd had with her last night, for the device.

Tamara.

Great. How would she explain the turmoil rolling through her to her boss's wife? Like she'd understand.

How did your date go?

Excellent, but the decision she had to make left her stomach churning. *Very well! Thank you for arranging it!*

So, r u going to c him again?

She longed to. Saying good-bye to everyone else kept her from saying yes. *I don't think it's possible.*

Y not?

He's not from around here. Not even close. She couldn't even hop on a plane to visit him for the weekend.

Her phone remained silent for several minutes. She lay back on her bed, memories of the previous night flooding her mind. She yearned to be filled again. Could she emulate the same intensity with her own toys? She reached into the drawer of her nightstand when her phone beeped again. This time, an email.

Danyka,

I don't mean to pry, but I'd like to know more about your date. If it went as well as you said, I'm sure you want to see him again. Perhaps you need more time off? Josh will understand. No matter what you decide, we will always be here for you.

Tamara

Would they understand? Time off meant a lifetime, not a week or even a year. She didn't know if she would ever return. However, she had the opportunity to try something new and different, something out of this world. And she would not pass it up. Forget the toys; she craved the real things. Volan's words echoed through her mind. *We will love you forever.*

And she wanted nothing but forever.

Grabbing her suitcase, she packed an outfit for every possible climate. Who knew where they'd end up? She'd spend the day writing timed emails to her friends and boss to inform them of her extended vacation, all while waiting for the night to come. She'd be gone by the time they received them.

A few more minutes.

As she spied the first star in the sky, her phone chimed. *Should I even look?*

But her curiosity got the better of her.

Tamara again.

If you happen to visit the Space Service space station, be sure to say hello to Carrie for me. I wish you all the best.

Space? How had she known? But a space station? Was that why Tamara's best friend had been absent from the wedding? She had so much to learn. And the message cleared away any remaining guilt she'd held onto.

Sitting on her bed, she looked to the darkened sky. "Galan and Volan, I choose you."

A light breezed blew her hair into her face. She sighed as fingertips slid across her shirt, tracing her tender nipples hidden underneath. Kisses trailed across the back of her neck. "Come to us."

Her limbs numbed and her body transported, leaving everything, including her suitcase, phone, and the clothes she'd been wearing, behind. The only thing she held onto was the handkerchief Tamara had left for her. For it belonged to her new lovers. When she opened her eyes, she lay back on the satin-covered bed, Galan and Volan, in all their naked glory, gazing down at her.

"I'm glad you've returned to us," Galan captured her lips for an intoxicating kiss.

Wrapping her arms around him, she vowed never to plan anything again. Who knew where this new life would take her?

Sudden Breakaway

Chapter One

Ms. Brown. Everyone knew her by that name, or at least those she tried to recruit for the Space Service did. For once, though, she wanted to be someone else, maybe herself. If she could shed the black designer suit and lose the title, she could simply be Paige.

The moment she'd signed the contract with the top-secret organization, she'd left Paige and the life she knew behind. Living in the shadows had been easy with her husband by her side, until agents destroyed the portal to the space station to keep terrorists from getting their hands on alien technology. Her husband—her only link to her old life—remained trapped there until the powers-that-be deemed it safe to repair the link.

She regretted agreeing to his traveling there for training while she remained on Earth, anxious about his welfare and resentful of the separation.

She continued to recruit for the Space Service, her work all she had to distract her from thinking of her faraway husband and empty bed. It wasn't until the divorce papers had been forwarded to her communicator, from space, that she'd regretted signing the lifetime contract. Her husband hadn't waited for her, choosing to bed some extraterrestrial bitch light years away.

She scanned her thumb across the ignition of her luxury sedan—only the best for members of the Space Service. None of it mattered anymore. She'd lost her enthusiasm for fostering relationships between Earth and the many worlds in the universe sustaining intelligent life. No, she wanted to stay on her home planet and find the love and happiness she'd thought she once had with her ex-husband.

She smirked, considering the possibility of her dream if she didn't find any new recruits soon. The Space Service would revoke her contract. Her last three prospects had turned down her offer of an "out of this world" work environment, not once, but repeatedly. Why hadn't she found the same strength, all those years ago to turn down the man in black who'd visited her and her husband? Though if she didn't recruit, what would she do for a living?

Foot on the brake, she glanced back at the house of her latest failure then pressed the button to shift into drive.

An honorably discharged former Marine with no ties to keep him grounded, he met every criteria for the ideal recruit. A fine male specimen, too. His dark, alluring eyes, smooth bald head, and well-defined muscles rippling under milk chocolate-colored skin stirred desires dormant inside her since she'd thumb-printed away her marriage.

She hadn't meant to arrive when he was in the shower, but would never apologize for the view of Mr. Tall-Dark-and-Handsome, wearing a thin white towel around his waist when he'd greeted her at the door. The image would remain forever implanted in her mind, the reference for every fantasy from that day forward. She should have thought to capture a digital image of him before she'd left, her forty-year-old brain known to dispose of information she'd rather remember.

Merging onto the highway, heading home, she sighed. Why could she no longer convince anyone to sign their life away? She'd contracted twenty men and women already. Had she lost her touch?

She hadn't had to head hunt these people herself, either. Her handler fed her all the important information regarding her prospects, including education, family, and any details she could use for leverage, such as a criminal record. All she had to do was persuade them they wanted the adventure of a lifetime. The thrill of the job had ended for her though. Perhaps the individuals she'd approached in the past few months had sensed her lack of enthusiasm.

Her first two nos, while they had no children or significant others, did have strong family loyalties. Jared Barnes, on the other hand, had no connections. His parents had both succumbed to cancer, and his sister died after a heart attack. He did have a niece and nephew, but they lived on the other side of the country with their father. What had kept him from saying yes? What key piece of information had she missed?

Steering toward the off-ramp, she exited the highway. Within two minutes, she pulled into her driveway. At least Jared didn't live far away. After her normal recruitment trips, she'd file her report through her tablet communicator while awaiting her flight. Tonight, though, after she sent off another notice of rejection, she would search the net for any gossip she'd missed about the sexy man who'd turned her down then crawl into a hot bath, picturing what he'd hidden under that towel. Moisture pooled between her legs as she rose from her car. *God, it's been so long.*

Screw the report and search. Paige yearned for an immediate release. She dropped her purse and communicator on the table by the front door and hurried to her bedroom. She removed her glasses, stripped her clothes off, and grabbed her big rubber friend. In the bathroom, she adjusted the flow of water to the ideal temperature and added some of her favorite bath oil. Never before had she been so eager to soak in the tub.

Steam rose off the hot water filling the claw-footed cast iron basin. Paige took a deep breath, smelling more than the lavender she'd added to the bath. No, the memory of his masculine scent surrounded her, saving all that was Jared for this moment.

She shuddered, imagining his large, firm hands gripping her waist. With a firm hold on her dildo, she slipped into the water, ready for Jared to star in her fantasy.

She sighed at the gentle force of his lips touching hers. His tenderness turned to urgency as he trailed a finger down to her already slick folds. She rocked her hips against him. Forget the foreplay; she wanted him deep inside her. Too much time had passed since she'd been properly fucked.

Grasping the edge of his towel, she yanked it from his waist. The soft cotton pooled at their feet. Jared drew her closer, his erection firm along her belly. Her cream trickled down her leg.

"Now, Jared. Take me, now."

He lifted her into his arms, lowered her into the tub, and then joined her in the warm water. The temperature of the liquid surrounding her served to amplify her desire.

Kneeling over her, his legs on either side of hers, he leaned down and captured her lips. But it wasn't enough. She yearned to be filled. Reaching between her thighs, he parted her swollen labia with his fingers, and used them to penetrate her heat.

She bucked underneath him, taking him even farther inside. Still, desperate for more, she clutched his hips. "Fuck me, Jared. Shove that huge cock into my pussy."

Nudging her legs apart with his knees, in one swift motion, he plunged deep inside her. Yesss.

He rocked in and out, hitting her G-spot with every thrust. Pressure radiated through her body as she joined him in the motion. Faster, faster....

She wanted the release, could think of nothing else. And in one blinding explosion, she climaxed, arching her hips toward the ceiling. Grabbing her dildo, she drove it in and out, riding the wave of her orgasm to the very end.

When she drew the rubber cock from her pussy, she wallowed against the emotional emptiness that consumed her. She pitched the faux penis across the room. She missed the way a lover could read what she wanted and needed even when she didn't know. But her life didn't allow for serious relationships. With so much money spent at the adult store over the past couple of years, she'd hoped the toys would be a suitable replacement. They had in the beginning, but now they no longer fulfilled her.

She left the tub, dried off, and then slipped into her silk robe. *Time to do something drastic.*

Œ

Jared shucked his towel and stroked his rigid cock. That woman made him hard every time she came to the door, trying to persuade him to sign up for the Space Service. Her claims had seemed far-fetched when she'd first approached him, yet his commander had confirmed her credentials, having been approached to join by another many years ago. While Jared would never add his thumbprint to the contract he'd read, he wouldn't mind if she stopped by to try and convince him again.

Ms. Brown, with her black blazer revealing a hint of cleavage and a skirt that showed the perfect curvature of her ass. When he'd answered the door fresh out of the shower and seen her on his porch, he'd gripped the door handle to hold himself back from yanking her inside and tearing off her fine-pressed suit.

He squeezed his balls—no time to jack-off. Dylan and Madison would arrive in an hour, and he had to take one last run through his house to get rid of any lingering dust bunnies before Children's Services appeared. No obvious dirt in the living room, he headed toward the kitchen, but his mind kept flying back to Ms. Brown.

She had the whole librarian thing going on, with her dark hair tied up in a bun and glasses resting on the end of her nose. Though, none of the women who worked at the local branch made his cock throb. Perhaps there was some truth to the naughty librarian tale. He wished.

Most women's version of naughty did not come close to his. While the whole BDSM club scene didn't appeal to him, he enjoyed a little bondage during foreplay. He'd spent months at a time deployed in the Middle East. While home, he appreciated the opportunity to date the pretty women who found a guy in uniform sexy. But once he fetched the cuffs, they bolted. They hadn't even wanted to use them on him.

Ms. Brown was no girl, though. No more than a couple years his senior, she exuded experience with her seductive glances, her posture that plunged her cleavage into his line of sight, and that damn wiggle of her ass as she sashayed back to her car. She could teach him a thing or two. He yearned for the chance to find out.

No, his next lay could no longer be at the forefront of his mind. In less than an hour, he would become the father figure to two impressionable young children. His sexual urges would have to take leave for the foreseeable future.

He'd been in his last month of deployment to Afghanistan when the call came in. And it took another day for his commander to reach him with the news. His brother-in-law had been killed in a car accident, leaving his niece and nephew orphans. And as much as he loved the Marine Corps—Semper Fi—he couldn't let the kids be raised by strangers. They had no other family left.

So, after he returned to the States, he contacted his lawyer and spent a couple of weeks obtaining guardianship of the children. He'd received his discharge papers, found a civilian position working as a desk jockey for the CIA through his contacts with the Marines, and bought a house suitable to raise two growing youngsters. After months of preparation, they were coming to live with him.

He glanced at his watch. Ten minutes until they arrived.

Shit! He'd wasted precious time thinking about Ms. Brown and his new life.

Grabbing a pair of jeans and a T-shirt, he yanked them on. Screw the boxers; his niece and nephew wouldn't notice. He peeked into their rooms to ensure they looked somewhat presentable. Would Children's Services take them back to California if his new living space didn't meet their standards?

He groaned. They weren't even at his house yet, and he'd been distracted. No more. Nothing would come before them. The children would be his priority. Everything he did would be for them, for the rest of his life.

☙

One month later….

What have I done? Jared yanked Dylan off the top of the fridge, holding him under his arm as the kid tried to wiggle free. "Superman can fly. You can't. If you jump from that high, you're going to get hurt."

Once the boy stopped squirming, Jared set him down and rushed over to his niece, who had decided to scribble on his white cell phone with a marker. "Madison, I know you love everything pink, but my phone does not need a makeover."

He grabbed the marker and she squealed, escaping under the table and down the hall clutching his phone. His morning had just begun. He couldn't even take a leak without the kids finding some kind of trouble. Yes, they went to daycare while he worked, but beyond the hours of nine to five, they were all his, and on weekends, he had no pardon. Why on Earth had he thought he could raise two preschoolers on his own?

The doorbell rang.

He glanced down the hall toward the bedrooms, where an ominous silence reigned. With the children quiet, they had to be plotting their next mission to destroy his sanity. Or perhaps they'd already started. Shrugging, he headed for the door, risking a future disaster to see who stood on his porch.

Dylan came charging at him, his dark eyes wide, reminding him of his sister when she was a child. "Someone's at the door. Who is it, Uncle Jared?"

The boy skidded straight across the slippery linoleum, his body slamming into Jared's knees.

Jared stumbled back, trying to regain his balance, and grasped the doorknob. The latch clicked open. Losing his footing again, he stumbled to the floor, his nephew landing on top of him. Groaning, he glanced up at the woman standing above him; his former commander's wife. "Can I help you, Mrs. Collins?

She lifted Dylan and balanced him on her hip. "From the look of things, I think I can help you." Slipping off her shoes, she lined them on the mat beside the rest of the footwear and continued into the house. "I'm giving you the day off."

What? He'd dreamed about time to himself since the day after his niece and nephew had arrived, but had accepted that would never happen. Not until the preschoolers were old enough to stay on their own, anyway.

He hopped to his feet, shut the door, and followed them into the living room. Madison had materialized out of nowhere, to join her brother, the pair of them sitting on either side of Mrs. Collins, their lopsided halos balancing atop their horns. Why couldn't they sit as still when no one else was around?

Slumping onto a chair, he leaned back and sighed. "How do you do it? How do you make them turn off?"

She chuckled. "I'm a guest. Trust me when I say kids always behave better around people they don't see every day. Back to why I'm here. My daughter says every time she sees you grocery shopping, you look ready to explode."

He didn't remember seeing the commander's teenage daughter, but any out-of-the-house excursions with the kids resulted in him trying to get back home as soon as possible. He tried to avoid running into anyone he knew. "I'm still getting used to having Madison and Dylan here. It's been quite a change."

The woman wrapped an arm around each child and snuggled them closer to her. "I always found I was a better mother when I had time away from my kids. I came back to them with a new focus and less stressed. But I had family around to take them here and there. Since you don't, I'm here to give you a break."

As much as he needed the respite, he worried about leaving his niece and nephew with someone else. What would they do to poor Mrs. Collins? "I don't know…."

"I raised three kids with Ernie in the Marine Corps. Two are away at college, and my baby is a senior in high school. I'll be fine."

He stared at the children, resentful of their sudden change in behavior. He needed to get away for a couple of hours. "Okay, you're right. I'll go get groceries and return right after."

She shook her head. "Not today. You're taking the rest of the day off. You need it."

"No, I—"

"Think of me as part of your team, Jared. That means you have to show some trust. I'll be by every Saturday to give you some time to yourself. Today, though, I've planned something extra special for you."

Oh God, what had she done?

The woman rose from the couch and handed him an envelope. "Ernie said you liked hockey, so we bought you a ticket to go see the hometown play this afternoon."

All right! He hadn't been to a match in...forever. But *a* ticket? "I'm going by myself?"

Her gaze shifted to the left before she returned eye contact.

Deception.

"No, your ticket will take you to a suite, and you'll have a space in the underground parking garage. Others will meet you there."

His heart raced in anticipation. Would he enjoy the game with his former squad? It had been so long since he'd seen any of them. "Okay, I'll go."

Mrs. Collins grinned. "Great. Go get ready. And be sure to dress nice."

Nice? For the guys? Yeah, right. It was hockey.

Chapter Two

Paige grabbed her shoulder bag from the passenger seat, and exited her car. The private parking pass she'd been granted added to the perfection of her date. A private suite at a hockey game, where she'd meet a—hopefully—gorgeous man for an afternoon of sexual pleasure. Could Madame Eve have delved any further into her mind in planning her ideal afternoon?

And the best part? She'd shed the confining black suit for a little red dress and matching stilettos. Though she'd left the daring and dangerous shoes in her bag to wear when she reached the suite. Running shoes suited concrete floors much better, and she had no idea how much walking would be involved on her way to her destination.

Closing the car door, she spun around to find a uniformed female concierge standing in front of her.

"Ms. Brown?"

She nodded, cringing inside. "I prefer Paige, but yes, that's me."

With a brief smile, the woman shook her hand. "Welcome to the Snyder Center. I have been asked to escort you to your suite. The other member of your party has not arrived yet."

Exactly as she'd wanted. She needed time to gain her bearings, assess her surroundings before her one-night, daytime stand arrived.

She'd learned to seek out possible breaches in security as part of her Space Service training. The last thing she needed was an overheard conversation between her and prospective recruits. Aliens and traveling through space using portals were subjects most of the population wasn't prepared to learn about. An all-out panic would not help the cause. As much as she yearned to be released from her contract, protecting herself and the organization she worked for from possible moles was one aspect of her job she would never be able to leave behind.

She dashed behind the concierge as the woman clip-clopped in her heels across the parking lot. Did the woman walk around the stadium every day in those things? Paige tried to avoid wearing anything higher than an inch. Today was special.

They reached a bank of elevators, and the concierge slid a keycard through the reader and the doors opened. Stepping inside, Paige clasped her stomach as it lurched. What had she been thinking when she arranged this date?

Jared.

Yes, the hunk of a man who'd increased her longing to leave the Space Service and have a normal life. She sighed. The star of her fantasies would not be her date. Would she be disappointed with the man Madame Eve chose for her? As long as he showed her a good time, made her forget her lack of a life for one day, she'd leave satisfied. And if all else failed, she'd watch the game, cheering for the visitors, her favorite team, a safe distance from the hometown crowd.

The ding of the elevator brought her back to the moment. She followed her escort down a long hallway until the woman stopped at one of the many doors. Were they all private suites? Soundproof? Security running in while she screamed with pleasure would ruin the moment.

The concierge handed her an envelope. "Your key is inside, along with everything else you'll need for the day. I will return to deliver your lunch, at twelve-thirty, right before the game. If you require anything else, dial the suite staff. The button is labeled on the phone."

Swiping her own card through the reader, the woman opened the door and smiled.

Paige walked into the suite, and then turned and handed her escort a tip. "Thank you."

The concierge nodded then left Paige on her own to get ready for the man who would make her forget her non-existent social life, even if for one day.

After removing her shoes from the bag, she placed it underneath the small desk. She took off her runners, wedged the heels on, and hurried to the bathroom to use the mirror, her date due to arrive in a couple of minutes. Spinning around, she took in every angle. Flawless, or at least, that's the image she wanted to portray to her date. He didn't need to know all of her faults if he'd never see her after their date. Would he arrive on time?

Yanking her fingers away from her mouth, she cursed the bad habit of nail biting she'd developed since the end of her marriage. She hadn't been this tense since her first day of training with the Space Service. Maybe watching the teams practice would calm her nerves and kill time before the rendezvous began.

Running her hand along the oak chair rail, she strolled toward the windows facing the rink. She stepped down the stairs, aiming for the front row of the theater-style seating. *Take it slow.* She didn't need to trip and do a face-plant into the window. Maybe it would have been easier if she'd taken the heels off, but what if her date walked in? She hoped the shoes would accentuate her ass and long legs, making her more appealing. If her date took one glance at her and walked out, she'd be crushed.

Lowering her seat, she sat down. Both teams practiced below, players coming onto the ice, stretching, and then skating around. Yum, would her date be a hockey player from the other team? A secret fantasy come true.

Her heart raced as locker room visions flooded her mind. Parading around in his hockey jersey, sex on the bench, in the showers.... Sudden warmth swallowed her up. She fanned herself. If she didn't control her overactive mind, she would need to pleasure herself before her date arrived. How embarrassed would she be if her date caught her fingering her pussy?

The door clicked open. She spun around in her seat to catch a glimpse of the man she'd spend the rest of the day with before he saw her. A rush of excitement fueled her fire. Her heart hammered in her chest.

He wore a jersey, but not from the team she cheered for. He wasn't a hockey player either. Her panties grew wet as she stared at his full, luscious lips, imagining them traveling all over her body, bringing her so much pleasure. Madame Eve could not have picked a better match for her. Every one of her recent fantasies would become reality.

She stood, grabbing the back of the chair to ensure her steadiness before making him aware of her presence. The shoes were bad enough, but her shaky legs—from anxious anticipation—could leave her humiliated.

The man glanced around the room. Would he be happy with her as his one-night stand? Could she satisfy him?

His eyes locked on hers.

"Hello, Jared."

His scowl came like a quick punch to the gut. He didn't want her. All hope she had for the date skittered away. His rejection stung almost as bad as the end of her ten-year marriage.

"I can't believe you stooped so low to get me to join the Space Service. And to get Mrs. Collins involved? This is the last time I'm going to tell you; I'm not interested."

"No." Shit, he had the wrong idea. "I'm here for a date. This has nothing to do with work."

His glare softened, yet his eyebrows remained drawn together. "A date?"

She chewed her bottom lip, her heart thudding. "Yes, I applied to a dating service.... The owner, Madame Evangeline, led me to believe my date would meet me here. I thought...?"

So much for her fantasies. She was too old for him, too different...not his type. Ducking in front of the seats seemed like the best option at the moment. Or leaping out the window.

"You thought I was your date."

She nodded, her chest constricting. No, she couldn't cry. The day was already bad enough without reducing herself to a blithering idiot in front of such an enigmatic man. With a deep breath, she regained some of her composure. "There must be some mix-up." She spun away from him. "I'll leave you to watch the game."

On her way to the door, she grabbed her bag. Before she left, Jared clasped her shoulders, electricity zinging through her body from his touch.

"Wait. Let me call home, check on the kids, and get this situation straightened out." He spun her toward him, brushing his hands down her arms. "I thought.... Doesn't matter. I'm glad you're here."

As much as she rejoiced in his change in attitude, the mention of children left her mind reeling. Nowhere in her notes had there been mention of Jared having any children. Had she missed that important piece of information, or had her handler left it out? The Space Service never sent her after prospects with offspring. Never. What the hell was going on?

ଓ

Jared hung up the phone, grinning. His niece and nephew were still alive. Mrs. Collins, too. That sneaky woman had led him to believe his buddies would meet him at the game. Instead, she and those fuckers had set him up on a blind date—a one-night stand through Madame Eve, who Ms. Brown also mentioned. Whoever Madame Eve was, the woman had to be magic. He couldn't have asked for a more perfect woman to be set up with—as if she'd been plucked from his deepest fantasies. God, his date exuded sexuality without even trying. And that red dress clung to every one of her delectable curves. Her long brown hair flowed down her back and across her shoulders in glossy waves. The right length to grasp while she....

Grrr.

If he understood the purpose of this date—a one-night stand—he would see every inch of the woman hidden underneath the scarlet fabric. His cock stirred at the thought.

Yet, he wore jeans and his hockey jersey. *Shit.* He should have listened to Mrs. Collins.

Would Ms. Brown—he didn't even know her first name—hold his attire against him, seeing as how she looked so damn hot?

He stepped forward, anxious to find out, and to touch her soft, creamy skin again. "I—"

She spun around, her brows knitted together. "I'm sorry, Jared. If I had known you had children, I never would have approached you about joining the Space Service. It's contrary to our policy to recruit parents."

Needing some contact with her, he rested a hand on her waist. *Oh, yeah.* "They're my sister's kids. I left the Marine Corps to take care of them when their father passed away."

She shook her head, her shoulders hunched. "Still." Her voice cracked. "I should have known."

Brushing his hand across her cheek, he yearned to see the sexy look she'd greeted him with. "I thought this was a date. Let's not talk about work. Besides, if you hadn't come after me, I would never have had the chance to fantasize about you."

Her posture relaxed as she raised her eyebrows. "You fantasized about me?"

No turning back. "Yes, and let me tell you, you were amazing."

A smile spread across her lips and into her mesmerizing brown eyes, sending shivers down his spine.

"Really?" Her sultry tone made him want to rip that red material off her. "Because you always left me satisfied in mine, every time."

His cock sprang to life, painful inside his jeans. He had to have her, feel her curvy body underneath his. No, not quite yet. "What's your first name, Ms. Brown?"

"Paige, why?"

"Because I needed to know before I did this." Wrapping one arm around her waist, he drew her next to him. He salivated as he took in her vanilla scent. *How ironic.*

He leaned forward and claimed her mouth, drawing her sweetness into his. Even better than he'd expected. And he wanted more. Lining her glossy lips with his tongue, he sought entrance. She moaned and opened for him, gripping his jersey. She ground her pelvis against his shaft. No point in denying what they both yearned for.

He reached around her back for the zipper of her dress. *Time to get it off.*

The zip of the teeth letting go was overshadowed by her soft sighs as he kissed his way down her neck. He dipped his hands under the straps to slide the outfit down. Without a bra, her breasts spilled over the seam of her dress. How he'd longed to touch them, lick them, like he wanted to do to every inch of her body. She arched her back, launching her creamy mounds even closer to his face. His. All his, at least for today.

Cupping both breasts, he licked one of her pebbled tips.

She cried out, throwing her head back. "Oh, Jared. Do you know how long it's been?"

As long as it had been for him? After leaving the Marine Corps, he'd spent all his time focused on getting custody of his niece and nephew, ignoring his sexual urges, relying on his fist. How many women wanted a guy with young ones attached? But would he want a female role model for them someday? Didn't matter. He had Paige's tit in his mouth and a hard-on that could break wood.

She twisted away from him. "Did you hear that?"

Fuck. "No. We're at a hockey game. It could be anything." He'd go mad if she stopped at every sound.

"I swear I heard someone at the door." She yanked up the straps and tucked her boobs back into the material.

No, no, no.

And then he heard it, too. The snap of the lock disengaging before the door opened. *Shit.*

He spun Paige around, hoping she looked presentable, and zipped her dress up. In front of him, she could hide the bulge in his pants. Yet he made sure she felt it pressing into the crack of her firm ass cheeks. Glancing over her shoulder, he clenched his fists as her cleavage heaved, resisting the urge to take them in his hands again.

The woman who'd escorted him up to the suite peeked in. "I have your lunches."

The woman had told him she'd return with their meals. When he'd seen Paige, though, he'd forgotten everything else. What were a few more minutes? As soon as the woman left, he'd strip the dress all the way off and leave it on the floor until he'd experienced all of Paige.

Chapter Three

The interruption came as a blessing, a way for Paige to slow things down. She wanted to get to know Jared, aside from what she'd read in her notes, which lacked some important information. And she hoped he'd learn more about her as well. She didn't jump into bed with a man on the first date—usually. Then again, she hadn't had time to meet guys. Hence, why she'd arranged the one-night stand.

With Jared, she wanted more than sex. She'd felt a connection from the first time he'd answered his door. The reason she'd returned to his house, in an attempt to recruit him a third and a fourth time. Unlike telephone solicitors, Space Service policy had her walking away and filing a report of refusal after two nos. For some reason, she'd gone back, hoping he'd change his mind, or maybe to see him again. And when she'd given up, he'd come back into her life.

For one day. Tomorrow, though, she would hop on a plane to visit her next prospect.

Jared slipped out from behind her to tip the concierge and then secured the chain across the door as the woman click-clacked down the hall. "I thought she would never leave."

He returned to stand behind her, his warm breath grazing the fine hairs on her neck. He swept his fingertips down her arms. "Now, where were we?"

As much as it pained her, she stepped away from him. "Why don't we eat? I'd hate to waste all the food."

He released her. "I'm sorry, I guess I misread you earlier. I thought you'd signed up for a one-night stand."

Guilt and hurt clenched her gut. Was that all he wanted, now that he knew why they were there? She spun around, unable to meet his gaze. "I thought, maybe, we could talk, get to know each other first."

Lifting her chin, he smiled down at her. "Really."

Was he making fun of her?

"Jared, I've never had a one-night stand before. I can't even remember the last time I went on a date." Talk about leaving herself vulnerable, but she had to make him understand.

"I'm okay with waiting, so long as you make me a promise." He grazed a thumb along her bottom lip, the simple gesture leaving her weak in the knees. She thought of taking it into her mouth, of taking him into her mouth. *Oh God.* She nodded, unable to voice any response.

"Promise me that before we leave, I'll have you out of that dress, and we'll continue what we started."

"Yes," she responded in a breathless whisper. How much longer could she resist him and her own urges?

He spun her around, resting his arm across her back, and guiding her to the rectangular bar table behind the theater seating. "Why don't you sit down, and I'll bring the food over." He squeezed her ass and strolled to the other side of the room.

She sighed, hopping up onto a high stool. Taking a deep breath, she attempted to regain some control. How would she look if she tackled him to the floor after telling him she wanted to wait? Desperate. And she was. For Jared, and no one else, making the wait that much more imperative. The entire day had to be right.

Jared arranged two plates on the table and then slipped onto the stool beside hers. "I must say, I'm glad I was set up with you." Resting his hand on her leg, he gripped her thigh. "I didn't know what you wanted, so I brought a little of everything. Feel free to eat off my plate if you see something you like." Instead of removing his hand to sample his own food, he toured farther up her leg, sliding under the skirt of her dress and grazing the wet silk cloth covering her delicate flesh.

Shit, the only thing she wanted to eat sat right in front of her. Six foot, three inches of mocha goodness. So much for biding her time. She could no longer contain herself. The food would still be there when they finished.

Crawling onto his lap, she wrapped her legs around the back of the stool, her dress riding up her thighs. She ran her hands along the front of his jersey. It had to come off. She needed to feel all of him.

He grabbed her wrists, lifting her arms above her head. "We're done eating, Paige."

The hunger in his eyes, along with his tight hold on her wrists, sent waves of anticipation zinging straight to her pussy. Nodding, she ground her hips against him. She wanted him, in this position, now.

"Good, 'cause I don't want to wait any longer. I'm not stopping until I've heard you scream my name several times."

When he ran his hands down her arms, she whimpered.

His eyes grew wide. "Did I do something wrong?"

She shook her head. "No, it's just...." God, how could she tell him what she wanted without turning him off? "It's ...I liked it when you held my wrists."

Showing off his white teeth, Jared grinned. "So, Ms. Brown likes a little bondage, does she?"

Her stomach clenched, and she wished she could read his mind. Would he find her too kinky for him? "I don't know. I've never tried before."

He captured her mouth in an erotic kiss, tasting her lips, drinking her in, all the while holding her hands behind her back. His cock brushed her stomach, making the wait for him unbearable.

Jared broke away, leaving her gasping for air. "How did she

know?"

"Who? Know what?" She didn't care, as long as he didn't stop.

"Mrs. Collins? Madame Eve? Whoever set us up. You see, I happen to enjoy having a woman handcuffed while I help her reach orgasm, over and over again. That is, if she's willing."

She creamed her panties right there on his lap. The thought of giving up total control to him sent flames of desire throughout her body. She would need to trust him. What was the worst that could happen?

He kissed her neck, his tongue grazing up to her earlobe. "Are you willing, Paige?"

"Yes." Her clit throbbed for attention. How much longer would he make her wait?

Releasing her wrists, he unzipped her dress and yanked it over her head. She wore nothing save for her thong and stockings. Aware of his gaze over her body, she shivered. Goosebumps spread across her skin, and her nipples hardened, as she waited for his touch.

"You're beautiful, Paige." He drew his finger across her body, starting from the top of her thong, up past her navel, and in between her breasts. He circled her erect buds with his thumbs. "I'm going to enjoy teasing you until you're begging me to let you come. Now, to find some restraints. I'll have to improvise since I don't have my cuffs with me."

Her breath caught. She couldn't respond, couldn't think straight, her mind focused on Jared's gentle touch.

He trailed his fingers down her sides and then her legs, slipping one under the edge of her thighs highs. "These will work perfectly."

In one swift movement, he scooped her up and carried her across the room. She wrapped her hands around his neck, startled by the motion. He laughed. "Afraid I'm going to drop you?"

"No." She loosened her grip. "You caught me by surprise."

He nestled his face into her neck, licking and sucking her sensitive skin. And as fast as he'd picked her up, Jared set her down in the cushioned leather chair. With a deep breath, she braced for his next move. The wicked smile on his face sent warmth straight to her core. Was she ready for what he had planned?

Jared fingered the edges of her stockings before rolling both down her legs, his touch like fire on her skin. "Are you sure this is what you want?" Clasping her wrists to the arms of the chair, he drew his tongue along her inner thigh, straight toward her pussy.

"Yes," she moaned, moisture flooding her already wet panties. "Oh God, yes."

"Good." He shifted her to the edge of the chair, touching his body.

Leaning forward, she met his mouth, moaning as his tongue played deliciously with hers. Skimming his hands away from her waist, he continued to feed the passion threatening to consume her from their kiss. And then the tightness around her wrists as Jared bound her to the chair. A new rush of excitement washed over her. She jerked back, struggling to breathe.

"You like being tied up, don't you?"

"Yes," she moaned. Even though she had submitted to him, she felt more alive than she ever had in her life.

"I can tell. You smell divine." He grazed her neck with kisses, planting them all the way down her body, and then focusing on the swell of her breasts. Cupping one in each hand, he brushed his thumbs over her sensitive nipples. Pure delight. And pure torture at the same time. She couldn't grab hold of him or strip him of the clothing he still wore. Not without breaking free of her restraints. And where was the fun in that?

"Now, if you want to stop, your safeword is...?"

"Chocolate," she whispered. "I want to use chocolate."

"Good. Are you ready, Paige?" The side of his mouth quirked in a sly grin.

She smiled back. "Not quite yet."

The confidence left his face, and he raised an eyebrow. "What do you mean? Did I tie you too tight?"

Her heart swelled at his concern for her, something she'd always wanted from her lovers. She'd never found that quality in any men before Jared, their only interest themselves. Even her husband. She'd thought that worked for her, being independent, even as a married woman. Now, she had her ideal fantasy man in front of her, and she planned to enjoy him as long as they were together. "No, I'm fine. I just want you to take your clothes off."

As quick as the jersey flew over his head, Jared's moxie seemed to return. The rest of his clothes fell to the ground, revealing a chiseled body that would make statues jealous. His broad shoulders, highlighting large pectoral muscles, left her longing to lean against him, wrapped in his arms after making love.

She blinked the thought away. Today was about sex. Nothing more. When she left, she wouldn't see Jared again. She had to keep her mind focused and enjoy every second they spent together.

She gazed farther down his body, finding her fantasy of what he hid behind the towel matched reality.

His thick cock stood rigid, like a giant chocolate ice pop, tempting her to take a taste. Yet she couldn't move, couldn't draw him any closer.

He knelt before her and spread her legs apart. "I'm going to have you, Paige."

Leaning forward, he brought his lips to hers. His hungry kiss engulfed her, leaving her mind numb, and her body aware of even the slightest touch. A tingling sensation filled her from head to toe, and her pussy clenched as he ran his digits down her stomach then through her slick folds. She sighed into his mouth. But he didn't let up, continuing his sweet invasion. Not until he thrust into her core did she draw back, gasping. It had been so long since any man had touched her, she'd forgotten how different it was from pleasure by her own devices.

"You're so wet, exactly the way I want you." He slipped a second finger inside, reaching up for her G-spot. And he found it, over and over again as he slipped in and out.

His thumb circled her clit as he leaned down to tug on her nipple with his mouth, intensifying her pleasure. She longed to reach out and grab him, to run her hands over his smooth head and down his back. With her wrists tied, she grasped the arms of the chair, so close to her release.

Jared removed his fingers, replacing them with his tongue. She thrust her hips into the air, overwhelmed by the sensations.

He pushed her back onto the chair. "It's too bad I don't have anything to tie your waist. I can't have you moving around like that when I'm trying to make this the best experience of your life."

She giggled. God, what was she, eighteen again? He did make her feel younger though, not affected by their eight year difference in age. At least not for today.

He threw her legs over his shoulders and grasped her hips. "Now, you won't be able to move as much."

Returning his attention to her pulsating core, he licked and sucked until she released in a blinding fury. She cried out, straining against her stockings, longing to touch Jared. He continued, lapping her juices until the chain of spasms subsided.

With ease, he untied her wrists. "Now, grab me," he said.

She reached past her legs for his cock, but he leaned back. "No, I mean, hold onto me. We're going to move."

Wrapping her arms and legs around him, she braced herself this time for his quick movements. He spun her around then propped her on the rim of a round pub table behind him. His attention seemed elsewhere as he glanced around the room, his eyebrows knit together.

"Is there a problem?" What could have changed his mood?

He returned his gaze to her and smiled. "I was wondering what we're going to do for protection. I wasn't expecting this to be a date. Though I'm really glad it is."

Brushing a hand across his cheek, she returned his smile. "Well, I knew. I have some condoms in my bag."

He left her clinging to the table. There was no way people could have eaten there—drinks only—not with the way she struggled to stay balanced. When he returned, she clasped his shoulders, thankful she'd managed to stay on.

He smirked. "I was gone for less than a minute."

She swatted him. "This table isn't meant to be sat on."

"No, but it will be a great place to take you. One of many."

She quaked at the thought. Jared spread her legs and moved between them. Tearing open the condom package, he rolled the latex over his engorged cock. Would he fill her as she'd fantasized? Even more? What if he didn't fit? She hadn't had sex since her husband left for the space station.

He drew her toward him and kissed her lips, her neck, while she dug her fingers into the wide expanse of his back. His shaft met her stomach. So close to fulfilling every dream she'd had over the last month.

"I want you in me, Jared. I can't wait any longer." With one hand around his neck, she reached down to position his tip at her entrance. *Oh God.*

He reclaimed her lips, fucking her mouth with his tongue as he thrust deep into her core, his cock filling her. Throwing her head back, she moaned. Even better than she'd imagined.

Grabbing her hips, he ground into her in a measured rhythm. The pressure built deep within, consuming her. Her pleasure intensified, and she filled with a need for something more.

No. She could never give more than one night and couldn't ask anyone for more than she could give.

Jared wrapped his arms around her and carried her over to the kitchenette counter. Propping her ass on the edge, he continued to fuck her, his movements more frenzied.

He stared deep into her eyes. "Oh, honey, I'm almost there."

His simple term of endearment sent her into oblivion. A cheer from thousands rang out all around them. Horns and buzzers echoed through the room. Red and blue flashed before her eyes as she rode the wild waves of complete satisfaction. With one final slamming thrust, Jared convulsed inside her, releasing a guttural roar.

He held her tight pressing his sweat-covered body to hers, his breathing ragged. "That's one goal I'll never forget."

☙

Paige sat on his lap, wearing only his jersey, her head resting on his shoulder. He wanted her there forever, couldn't imagine being without her now that he'd experienced her. Would it all seem like a dream the next day?

He fingered her long brown hair. She fit snug in his lap, as if she were meant to be there. How was he going to say good-bye in a couple of hours when she already occupied his last thoughts every night before he fell asleep? With all of the recent changes in his life, he couldn't afford to let a good woman go. It wasn't as if he had a lot of time to date. Would she understand why he couldn't wine and dine her every night, take her out to sporting events and the theatre like he should? That gourmet at his house meant chicken fingers and macaroni and cheese?

He tried to focus on the game, but his mind kept wandering to the gorgeous creature he held in his arms. Glancing up at the scoreboard, he realized his team hadn't scored yet. He squeezed Paige. "Well, that sucks. The memorable goal was for the other team."

"I think that makes the moment even better." She spun in his arms and smiled up at him.

Loosening his grip, he gasped. "Don't tell me you're a fan of the other team."

"Yep, since 1991."

He rolled her off his lap and onto the chair beside him, pretending to be disgusted, yet still holding her so she didn't fall to the floor. "I can't believe I had sex with a fan of the visiting team. And you're wearing my jersey. I'll have to disinfect it."

She rose to her feet in front of him, hands on her hips, and puffed her chest out. The motion made him want to rip the jersey off and have her again.

"I can't believe you would hold that, of all things, against me."

He would hold none of their differences against her, because he didn't care. She was Paige, the beautiful woman he wanted to spend more time with. If she agreed. Scooping her into his arms, he laughed at the same wide eyes and gasp of shock as the last time he'd surprised her. The look faded, and she burst into a fit of giggles. How could he give her up? They'd had hot sex, and he could see beyond that. Could she?

He sat back down, holding her in his arms. "Paige, I want to see you again after this. I know we both have other commitments in our lives, but I'd like to give it a try, see where this goes."

Her entire body stiffened as she leaned away from him. "I...I can't."

A tear trickled down her cheek. He wiped it away with his thumb, trying to ignore the vices around his heart.

Shit. He hadn't expected that answer.

"It's the kids, isn't it?" He couldn't blame her, couldn't expect any woman to take on two children after the first date.

"No. Yes. It's just with the Space Service, I can't commit to anything, anyone. I don't want to hurt them, or you." She reached down and stroked his cock. "Let's not talk about that."

She slipped off his lap, and kneeled in front of him. As she fondled his balls, she sank her mouth over his shaft. He groaned. It felt so good, he forgot what they'd been talking about.

Chapter Four

Paige sank into one of the chairs beyond customs at McCarron International Airport in Las Vegas. Back row, third from the left, her usual, and—thank goodness—unoccupied seat. From there, she had the perfect vantage point to see everyone coming and going. Reaching inside her shoulder bag for her tablet, she sighed. Another "no" to the Space Service, leading to another rejection report, one that should have been prevented before she even arrived in Las Vegas. Her prospective recruit, Claire Donovan, had answered the door, a newborn baby in her arms. Her handler should never have sent her to visit the woman. Now, she'd have another rejection on her record. Was the person feeding her information slacking, or trying to get her fired? She wanted to leave the Space Service, but not as a result of someone else's inefficiencies. She was too professional to allow someone to take her down, or to try to break her contract. The contact was why she'd had to say good-bye to Jared after the hockey game and their forever-memorable elevator ride down to the parking garage.

As soon as she'd driven away from him at the stadium, the void of loneliness had swallowed her. Such was the life she'd signed up for. No, she'd signed up with her husband, and he'd left her lonely and bound by a contract that left her no time to find someone else who might love her. Jared could have been that guy, if she'd had the chance to find out.

Opening the report document, she cursed her ex and her contact. It was all she could do to remain seated rather than leaving the airport and the Space Service forever. Where would that get her? Her employer had access to technology that would lead them straight to her no matter where she went. No, she was destined to be alone for the rest of her life, her only chance of a connection to any man through a one-night stand.

Her tablet beeped, indicating an incoming video call. The link, her handler. She'd never seen the person face-to-face, never knew if she'd had the same one from the beginning. With a deep breath, she prepared to give him or her a piece of her mind.

Grabbing her bag, she stood, already in search of a secluded spot to have the upcoming conversation. Rage boiled from deep within her, and she didn't need to be revealing secrets kept from the world in anger. In a corner away from the hustle and bustle, she hit connect.

Her ex-husband's face flashed onto the screen.

"Zane?" *What the hell?* He was the last person she wanted to see. Realization dawned on her. Her ex was the idiotic person trying to ruin her career.

"Hello, Paige. How did your recent recruiting assignment go?" His toothy grin, even on screen, made her skin crawl.

"You asshole. You know damn well how it went." Her knuckles grew white as she gripped the screen. He'd sent her to recruits guaranteed to reject her offer. Why? "Care to tell me why you've been feeding me misinformation?"

He raised an eyebrow. "Simple. I want you out of the Space Service. My Draseda is young and vibrant, and eager to take your position."

So that was her replacement's name. An alien as a recruiter? Yeah, right. But she'd never admit how much she wanted to leave her career behind. Not to him. "I signed a contract. And how is that possible? You're both on the space station."

"Oh, Paige, you've really been kept in the dark."

His chuckle grated on her nerves. What was he talking about?

"My dear ex-wife, I've been back for months. I'm not going to tell you how, as you don't have the clearance. I've been your handler for that long, too."

Around the same time she'd received her first rejection. Damn. Wouldn't that look suspicious to the Space Service? They knew the two of them had been married. "Yes, but the contract?"

"I can get you out of it."

Her heart skipped a beat. Had she heard his whispered words correctly? "You what?"

"I said, I can make the contract null and void. I kept hoping you would do so yourself, get pregnant by one of the young studs you kept recruiting before I became your contact. I mean, I can't see why they wouldn't be interested in a fox like you. Isn't your biological clock ticking? Or are you that dedicated to your job?"

God, what had she ever seen in that man? Had he always been such an insensitive ass? With a deep breath, she reined in her anger. It would do her no good to explode on him. Not when he held her chance for freedom. "How?"

"You leave that up to me. All you have to do is give me the word."

"And where will that leave me?" No matter what, there would be repercussions from her leaving the Space Service. If it were that easy, she would have walked away as soon as her marriage had ended.

"Your house, vehicle, and all communication systems will revert back to Space Service property. Your belongings will be placed in a storage locker, and an agent will meet you at Dulles with the key and to collect your tablet. Your salary for the rest of the year, as well as the agreed upon severance stated in your contract will be deposited in your bank account. Then you're on your own."

It all sounded too good to be true. Sure, she'd be homeless and without a job. Her bank account could handle that. There had to be something else, some other obstacle she couldn't think of. "What's the catch?"

"You never worked for the Space Service. You've been out of work for fifteen years."

Yes, that would be tough to explain.

"Say the word, Paige."

She drummed her fingers against the bottom of the tablet. If she ever met a man like Jared again, she wouldn't have to leave him behind. She'd be able to have a relationship. Was it worth giving up the last fifteen years? She drew in a deep breath. "Yes, Zane, I want out."

"Done. It was nice knowing you."

The screen went blank. She pressed the power button, but the tablet would not work.

Oh God, what have I done? Where am I going to go? She should have asked for more time to decide. Without her tablet, life as she knew it had ended. She was free, but completely alone in the world.

☙

Jared jerked back on his lead foot. As anxious as he was to get home, he didn't need to get a speeding ticket. Not only were Mrs. Collins and the kids waiting for him, he also had an interview with a possible housekeeper in five minutes.

He hadn't planned on allowing another person into his fold, but his niece and nephew kept him on the move. When he finally got them into bed at night, he wanted to relax, not have to worry about vacuuming, and laundry. Mrs. Collins had convinced him to place a classified ad in the paper, but only one person had responded. The woman wasn't even qualified; her experience keeping her own home clean.

From his short conversation with her, there'd been something familiar, something telling him to give her a chance. He hoped he wouldn't live to regret following Mrs. Collins's advice again.

The woman meant well. But after his one-night stand experience, his nights had been lonelier than ever. He longed to have someone to share his bed with and his love. No, not just anyone. Paige. He couldn't get her out of his mind, though he knew he would never see her again. She haunted him, came to him in dreams during which he relived every erotic moment of their time together, from her mouth gliding down the length of his cock as the crowd cheered, to her screams as she experienced orgasm during their elevator ride. His wrist always got a workout before he fell asleep. And now, as he steered into his driveway, his cock strained inside his pants, yearning for release. What a way to meet a prospective employee.

She stood on his porch, her back to him, hand lifted to ring the doorbell. He gazed upon the soft curves of her body, her long, wavy brown hair. So memorable, even without the black suit or the skimpy red dress. Impossible. She'd said her life belonged to the Space Service. Why would she be on his doorstep? And the woman on the phone had said her name was Piper. Was he hanging on to a false hope? *Only one way to find out.*

He yanked the car door open and bounded up behind her. "Can I help you?"

She spun around to face him, a grin spreading across her lips.

He gasped. *No, it can't be her.*

"Hello, Jared." His name rolled off her tongue, sounding sexier than any woman who'd tried to pick him up as a Marine.

"Paige? You're here?" Or was his imagination playing tricks on him?

She reached up and stroked the side of his face, her simple touch fanning the fire deep within him. God, how he'd missed her. "Is this another recruiting visit, because you know I'll never join the Space Service. I'm responsible for two active preschoolers."

"Space Service, what's that?" She stared at him as if she had no idea what he was talking about. "No, I'm here for the housekeeping position. And I've always wanted to have children of my own. Maybe one day."

"You're a housekeeper now? I thought—"

"I've been out of work for fifteen years." She winked at him. "Without any experience, I can't expect to find a salaried position."

"Wait." *Shit!* How had he not recognized her voice over the phone? "You said your name was Piper."

"Yes, I did. I wanted to surprise you, and I see I did."

He groaned as she stood next to him and rubbed the length of his cock.

"Though, I'm hoping this was for me, and not someone else."

If she only knew how often she'd been on his mind over the last two weeks.

"You, oh God, you." He pressed his body to hers, backing her against the front door. Claiming her mouth, he reveled in her sweetness. As much as he desired her, the ache that had settled on his heart receded with every stroke of his tongue. He'd hoped for something more. And with her here.... Dare he think it possible?

The door opened behind Paige. Grasping her shoulders, he held her steady so she wouldn't fall into his foyer. Mrs. Collins's wide eyes met his. "I'm back, and my interviewee is here as well."

"I see that, though I didn't think the interview would be so intimate."

He chuckled at her questioning glance. "It turns out I know her." He smiled at Paige before spinning her around to face the older woman. "Paige, I'd like you to meet Mrs. Collins, one of the women responsible for setting us up."

Paige waved. Even though he couldn't see her face, he smiled at her sudden sheepish posture. Ms. Brown, former Space Service recruiter, was embarrassed?

Mrs. Collins winced, her face reddened. "I'm sorry I interrupted. I just thought you needed help bringing in the groceries. I'll...I'll gather Dylan and Madison and take them to the back yard while you give Paige a tour of the house." She took a step back and paused. "I can't stay much longer today, as Ernie and I have plans, but next Saturday, I can watch the kids late into the night if you'd like."

"That would be great, Mrs. Collins," he called to her retreating form. "Thank you."

He kissed the top of Paige's head then reached for her hand to guide her into his house. "Welcome to my home. If you're lucky,

I'll let you see my cuffs."

She giggled. "I'd like that. Maybe tonight?"

"Yes." Hallelujah! Ms. Brown had returned to his home. And in the future, if things went well, it would be hers, too.

~ABOUT THE AUTHOR~

Jessica Subject started writing to encourage her daughter to read. Now she writes to keep herself grounded. Although she reads many genres, she enjoys writing Science Fiction Romance the most and believes everyone in the universe deserves a happily ever after. She lives Southwestern Ontario, Canada with her husband and two kids and loves to hear from anyone who has enjoyed her stories.

You can visit Jessica at:
jessicasubject.com

www.ingramcontent.com/pod-product-compliance
Lightning Source LLC
LaVergne TN
LVHW050636100826
845148LV00011B/1884

* 9 7 8 1 6 1 3 3 3 3 5 7 0 *